MURDER
ON THE TROPIC

MURDER
ON THE TROPIC
A HUGH RENNERT MYSTERY

TODD DOWNING

COACHWHIP PUBLICATIONS

Landisville, Pennsylvania

Murder on the Tropic by Todd Downing
Copyright © 2012 Coachwhip Publications
Introduction © 2012 Curtis Evans
No claim made on public domain material.

ISBN 1-61646-150-0
ISBN-13 978-1-61646-150-8

Cover Image: Marigold © Prakit Na Somboon

CoachwhipBooks.com

CONTENTS

INTRODUCTION
CURTIS EVANS

"Mr. Downing is a born detective story writer."
—Edward Powys Mathers ("Torquemada"),
review of Todd Downing, *Vultures in the Sky* (1935)

THE RICHNESS AND DIVERSITY of American genre writing during the Golden Age of mystery fiction (c. 1920 to 1939) is much under-appreciated today. Golden Age mystery readers could choose from a wide variety of literary dishes, be it the tough stuff of the hard-boiled boys (most famously Dashiell Hammett, Raymond Chandler and James M. Cain), which has long received the lion's share of the attention that scholars have granted American Golden Age crime writers; the psychological suspense (or HIBK—Had I But Known—as it was once disparaged) of Elisabeth Sanxay Holding, Mary Roberts Rinehart, Mignon Eberhart and Leslie Ford; the urban sophistication of Rex Stout, Patrick Quentin and Rufus King; the madcap humor of Phoebe Atwood Taylor and Craig Rice (the latter making the tail end of the Golden Age); the eccentric extravaganzas of Harry Stephen Keeler; the police procedurals of Helen Reilly; the courtroom dramas of Erle Stanley Gardner; or the magnificent baroque puzzles of S. S. Van Dine, Ellery Queen, Anthony Abbot, John Dickson Carr, C. Daly King and Clyde B. Clason.

This listing of authors just scratches the surface of American mystery writing in the years between the two world wars. So many accomplished mystery writers from the period have undeservingly fallen into obscurity. One such individual is Todd Downing, the Golden Age chronicler of fictional murders in Mexico.

Todd Downing was born in 1902 in the town of Atoka, Choctaw Nation, Indian Territory (soon to be Oklahoma). Though one-eighth Choctaw and, like his father Samuel (Sam), an enrolled member of the Choctaw Nation, Todd Downing had what in many ways was a traditional, early twentieth century small town American upbringing. Both Todd's father Sam and his mother Maud were staunch churchgoing Presbyterians and Republicans and Todd was brought up according to the proper precepts of these two orthodoxies.

Yet the Downing family of Atoka was unusual in its great love of reading. From an early age Todd Downing could be found in nooks and corners of the family's two-story foursquare house with his nose buried in books. He particularly loved romantic tales of adventure, played out in settings around the globe. Beginning with Sir Walter Scott's and H. Rider Haggard's colorful sagas of derring-do, Todd moved on, in his teenage years, to crime and mystery, in the form of the short story collections of Arthur B. Reeve, creator of the virtuous scientific detective Dr. Craig Kennedy, and the novels of Sax Rohmer, creator of the diabolical criminal mastermind Dr. Fu Manchu.

After Todd became a student at the University of Oklahoma in 1920, he soon discovered Edgar Wallace, the awesomely prolific English king of the thriller. Todd devoured Wallace shockers at a prodigious rate. (His library of books, bequeathed at his death in 1974 to Southeastern Oklahoma State University, included sixty-five Wallace novels and short story collections, as well as Wallace's autobiography and biography.) Yet as the 1920s progressed, Todd, like many bright people in his day, became increasingly interested in fair play detective fiction, where the point is not emotional jolts but cerebration: the reader tries to solve the mystery for her/himself through clues provided within the text by the author. Over the decade of the twenties Todd purchased detective novels and short story collections by Anthony Berkeley, Earl Derr Biggers, Lynn Brock, G. K. Chesterton, Mignon Eberhart, Rufus King, Marie

Belloc Lowndes, Baroness Orczy, Mary Roberts Rinehart, T. S. Stribling and S. S. Van Dine.

Between mysteries Todd managed to find time to qualify for his B.A. and M.A at the University of Oklahoma, as well as to take classes in Spanish, French and anthropology during summers spent at the National University of Mexico. In 1928 OU hired the young Atokan as an instructor in Spanish. (Todd was fluent in five languages: English, Choctaw, Spanish, French and Italian.) In addition to teaching his OU classes and conducting summer tour groups in Mexico, Todd continued voraciously reading both detective novels and crime thrillers; and in 1930 he began reviewing mysteries of all sorts in the literary pages of Oklahoma City's *Daily Oklahoman*. Especial favorites of Todd's in the mystery line were Agatha Christie, Dorothy L. Sayers, Ellery Queen, John Dickson Carr, Dashiell Hammett, Mary Roberts Rinehart, Mignon Eberhart and additional worthy writers who likely are less familiar to many today: Anthony Abbot, Rufus King, H. C. Bailey, Eden Phillpotts and Anthony Wynne (for more on Todd Downing's mystery fiction reviews see my book *Clues and Corpses: The Detective Fiction and Mystery Criticism of Todd Downing*).

Encouraged by an older colleague at the University of Oklahoma, Professor Kenneth C. Kaufman, Todd Downing wrote his first detective novel in 1931, not long after he had begun contributing mystery fiction reviews to the *Daily Oklahoman*. Eventually published in 1933, *Murder on Tour* introduced Todd's most important series detective, United States Customs Service agent Hugh Rennert, who would appear in seven detective novels between 1933 and 1937. (A Hugh Rennert novella, probably written by Todd in 1932, was published in 1945.) Besides *Murder on Tour* these are: *The Cat Screams* (1934), *Vultures in the Sky* (1935), *Murder on the Tropic* (1935), *The Case of the Unconquered Sisters* (1936), *The Last Trumpet* (1937) and *Night over Mexico* (1937). All six of these later novels now have been reprinted by Coachwhip Publications.

The Hugh Rennert detective novels are primarily set in Mexico (the one exception being *The Last Trumpet*, where the action ranges from Cameron County, Texas to the Mexican state of Tamaulipas). Todd Downing's authoritative and fascinating use of Mexico as a setting in his detective novels makes him one of the most important regionalist mystery writers of the Golden Age and is his most significant contribution to the genre. Additionally, the Rennert novels are graced with teasing fair play puzzle plots, stylish writing and interesting characterizations. Hugh Rennert himself is a notable detective, modest, middle-aged, self-reflective and somewhat melancholy, yet resolute and determined. ("A good kind man," one character calls him in *Night over Mexico*, and he is.) Hugh Rennert is fascinated with Mexico and *vacilada*, the mirthfully stoic attitude of the country's people toward life and death; and over the course of the series Todd Downing explores what might be termed the metaphysical relationship of Rennert and Mexico in interesting ways. We learn a lot about both a man and a country.

After 1937 Todd Downing wrote two more detective novels, both with a different series detective (Texas sheriff Peter Bounty, introduced in *The Last Trumpet*): *Death under the Moonflower* (1938) and *The Lazy Lawrence Murders* (1941). He also published the work which he considered his crowning achievement as a writer, a non-fictional study of Mexico, *The Mexican Earth* (1940; reprinted by the University of Oklahoma Press in 1996). Sadly, Todd's attempt in the 1940s to write a mainstream historical novel about Mexico came to naught. Todd had resigned as an instructor at the University of Oklahoma in 1935 in order to devote himself professionally to writing, but after 1941 he would never publish another novel—indeed, after 1945 he never published any fiction of any kind again. In the 1940s Todd found employment as an advertising copy writer in Philadelphia. One of his ads, the tongue-in-cheek mystery homage "The Case of the Crumpled Letter," was chosen in 1959 as one of the 100 greatest advertisements.

In the 1950s Todd returned to the teaching profession, taking posts at schools in Maryland and Virginia, but after the death of his father in 1954 he returned to Atoka to live with his octogenarian mother and teach Spanish and French at Atoka High School, from where he had graduated thirty-five years earlier. After the death of Todd's mother in 1965, Todd lived on alone in the old family home until his own demise in 1974. The professional highlight of his later years was his appointment as Emeritus Professor of Choctaw Language and Choctaw Heritage at Southeastern Oklahoma State University (then Southeastern State College). Reflecting Todd's continued interest in his Choctaw heritage were his series of lessons in the Choctaw language, *Chahta Anampa: An Introduction to Choctaw Grammar*, and his historical pageant play about the Choctaw Nation, *Journey's End*, both of which were published in 1971, forty years after he penned his first detective novel.

Todd Downing is buried beneath a simple headstone in Atoka, the place of his birth. Fittingly, his writing lives after him.

1
FORECAST OF MURDER

"THIS WEATHER PROBABLY accounts for it. It's got my nerves on edge." Edward Solier frowned at an inkwell of Mexican onyx on the top of his desk. His thin wiry body, far back in a leather-cushioned swivel chair, had a false appearance of ease, for his small tanned hands were clasping and unclasping nervously over his abdomen.

He glanced at a tiny calendar to the left of the ink well and said crisply: "June twentieth. A cool spring and now the beginning of what looks like an unusually hot summer. Damned peculiar weather for this part of Texas, Mr. Rennert."

The man across from him sat quietly with folded arms. His pleasant middle-aged features expressed only polite attention but his clear brown eyes, gray-flecked, studied the other thoughtfully.

"Yes," he agreed. He was considerably puzzled by this summons to Solier's office in one of San Antonio's newest and most pretentious buildings, by the uneasy tension of the gray little man's manner, by his irritating delay in coming to the point.

Solier opened a drawer and pushed forward a box of cigars. Rennert took one and Solier held out a lighter. He kept it in the air for a moment afterwards, uncertainly. With the other hand he took a cigar and thrust it into his mouth, biting off the end with a click of his teeth.

There was a brief interval of silence as the two thin spirals of smoke rose into the hot still air. Far below the afternoon traffic of San Antonio was a subdued though insistent murmur.

Solier's features seemed to relax under the influence of the tobacco. One side of his mouth moved in a smile.

"I understand that early spring freeze ruined a lot of citrus fruit
down in the Lower Rio Grande Valley," he remarked.

Rennert's eyes were on the smoke.

"Yes," he nodded. "It did a great deal of damage."

"Hit your hundred and twenty acres rather hard, I suppose?"

So that's it! Rennert said to himself. He had heard of such tac-
tics before. Promoters would sell land at high prices (as Solier had
sold to him) then would buy it back at the first moment of discouragement on the part of the purchaser—for a much lower price. An
offer, Rennert reflected, would have found him an eager listener,
had it come in March, after that unexpected, almost unprecedented
cold wave. Now, after the expense of replanting . . .

"I've been wondering," Solier went on without waiting for a
reply, "if you'd like to make up for the damage the cold did by under-
taking a little mission for me."

Rennert paused in the act of tapping his cigar against the side
of an ashtray of the same milky-gray onyx as composed the rest of
the desk-set. His eyes met Solier's.

"What kind of a mission?" he asked, the wariness instilled by
his profession asserting itself.

"I own an interest in an hacienda down in Mexico, about one
hundred and twenty-five miles southeast of Monterrey. We're in a
bit of difficulty there. I know enough about you to feel that you're
the man to handle it—if you'll undertake it."

"Thanks," Rennert said, "but go on. Why?"

Solier unclasped his hands and moved the cigar to the other
side of his mouth.

"I remember with a great deal of pleasure that trip we took
down into the Valley, when you decided to buy that land. Then,
too, I've heard a lot about you from Mr. —." (He named a grizzled
superior of Rennert's in the Treasury Department at Washington.)
"I feel sure that a leave of absence could be arranged, if you say
so. You see," a forefinger toyed with an onyx-backed blotting-
pad, "I have political connections. As to your fee," he paused for a

fraction of a second, "I can promise you that it will be decidedly worth your while."

Rennert's eyes went to the window, followed a frothy white cloud that was floating lazily across the sky.

The sky and the cloud fitted, somehow, the mood that had come upon him with increasing frequency of late. It was the recurrence of this mood (combined with the mirror's reflection of gray hairs creeping remorselessly up from his temples) that had led him to the purchase of the citrus farm in the Valley. It had been a gamble, of course, but it offered a chance for a steady income, retirement from an arduous occupation, and unhurried indulgence in many long-fondled desires.

"Suppose," he said, "that you be a little more explicit, Mr. Solier. You haven't yet told me the nature of this mission."

Solier shifted his position in the chair and threw one leg across the other.

"The idea," he spoke through clamped teeth, "was to build a big hotel a day's drive south of Monterrey on the new Pan-American Highway to Mexico City. We had what we thought was definite information that the road would go through a certain tract of land. The family that owned it was living in Mexico City and doing nothing with it. Three of us—George Stahl, Tilghman Falter, and I—formed a company to buy it and build the hotel. We sold shares." He paused and looked inquiringly at Rennert. "I believe you were approached on the subject?"

Rennert nodded but said nothing.

"Well," Solier went on, "the route of the highway was changed to the eastward, to go through Linares and Victoria, and we were left with this isolated property on our hands."

"I was sure that would happen," Rennert said. "I made a few inquiries in Monterrey and learned that it was practically certain the road would not go through the country you had in mind."

Solier's eyes fastened themselves on his face. His teeth sank a bit deeper into the cigar.

"If we'd had the benefit of your information we'd have saved a lot of money," he shrugged. "As it is we've got the hacienda—Flores, it's called—and don't know what to do with it. With irrigation it could be made into profitable farm land, I suppose, but none of us want to undertake that. We have bought back most of the shares for what we could afford to pay, so that we could get rid of it. It wasn't much, because the purchase of the land and the legal entanglements took most of our capital. Falter has stayed down there until things are settled. Two weeks ago Stahl and I went down to look the place over and make some decision. We'd succeeded in buying up all the shares except one block." He tapped the end of his cigar gently against the tray and didn't look up as he said: "Stahl died while we were there."

The flat toneless way he said it made Rennert glance at him sharply.

Solier was continuing: "His interest went to his stepson, Mark Arnhardt, who had accompanied us on the trip." He looked at Rennert again. "I want you to persuade the person who owns the last block of shares to sell. Even if you have to pay the full purchase price, do so. I'm getting tired of the whole deal, and am willing to take a loss in order to get out of it. As I told you at the beginning, this sultry weather probably accounts for my feeling. I want a vacation—without any worries."

"Who is this person who owns the last block of shares?"

"A Miss Fahn, Bertha Fahn. She's an old maid from Austin. She invested a small sum of money and now won't sell. Just why I don't know. She has been staying at the hacienda, making some kind of a study of plants and flowers. It's a god-forsaken place to live but she hasn't budged since she bought the shares."

Rennert's thoughts were busy. He wondered just what was behind Solier's proposal. Surely, if it was merely a question of persuading a maiden lady to sell her interest . . .

"Since Mr. Falter is at the hacienda, why can't he buy the shares from her?" he asked.

"I talked to him yesterday." Solier must have caught the questioning look on Rennert's face for he hastened to explain: "We have a short-wave radio set at the hacienda so that we can be in constant communication. He's been in bad health lately, something wrong with his stomach, and probably hasn't been very diplomatic. He says that she flatly refuses to consider any offer that he makes. I gather that he has rather antagonized her."

"And that is the extent of my duties—to persuade her to sell these shares?"

Solier cleared his throat.

"Well, there's another matter, too. Probably doesn't amount to anything, but it has Falter worried. It's about the water."

"The water?"

"Yes, the drinking water. There are some springs up in the mountains above the hacienda that we depend on for our supply. The rainy season has been so long in starting, however, that the springs are beginning to dry up. Falter has been having the drinking water brought up from Victoria in bottles. Someone on the hacienda, it seems, has been emptying these bottles."

"After they are brought to the hacienda?"

"Yes. Every night a bottle or two is emptied. Falter thinks someone is trying to force the occupants of the place to move. I'd like to have you look into this matter, too, if you will." Solier's eyes fixed themselves on Rennert's face with a steady appraising directness. "You see the situation," he said. "It's impossible for me to get away at present. Will you go?"

Rennert clasped his hands behind his head and stared thoughtfully out the window.

Solier watched him for a moment then opened a checkbook. He tore out a check, already made out, and passed it across to him. "For expenses," he said.

Rennert glanced at the check, was mildly surprised at the amount. He made no motion to take it.

He was practical enough to know that this represented an opportunity to repair the damages to his citrus fruit along the Rio Grande, even to build a modest house there. He was also practical enough to realize that he was going into the affair, if he went, almost blindfolded. For he was certain that Solier was holding something back. No one was going to pay the price that Solier was offering for anything as trivial as his services promised to be. At the same time a whisper at the back of his mind told him that this very element of uncertainty appealed to him, that there was lurking there an unacknowledged hope that the humdrum routine of existence might be broken again.

"There are a few questions I'd like to ask," he said.

"Sure, anything you want to know." By the way Solier said it Rennert knew that his consideration of the offer had betrayed his interest.

"First, how many people are staying at the hacienda?"

"Eight."

"Would you mind running over the list?"

"Not at all. There's Falter, and Miss Fahn, and Mark Arnhardt, Stahl's stepson, whom I've mentioned. Then there are the Tolmans, husband and wife. He's a young architect whom we engaged to draw the plans for the hotel when it was first projected. He's suffering from tuberculosis and has stayed on at the hacienda in the hope that the climate would help him. Esteban Flores is still there, I think. He's a young Mexican whose airplane crashed near the hacienda about two weeks ago. He has been trying to get parts to repair it from Mexico City but doesn't seem to be having much luck."

"I understood you to say," Rennert interposed, "that the hacienda was named Flores. Any connection?"

"Yes, it used to belong to his family. We bought it from his father."

"And how long has this group been there?"

"The Tolmans about two months, Miss Fahn about a month, Flores two weeks. Arnhardt went down with Stahl and myself, came back with Stahl's body, then returned."

"You mentioned eight people. Who are the other two?"

"Oh, old Miguel Montemayor and his wife. They're fixtures at the place, act as sort of caretakers."

Rennert thought a moment.

"All of them were present at the time of Stahl's death, then?"

Solier frowned.

"What makes you ask that?" His eyes were fixed on Rennert's face.

"I was merely wondering about Stahl's death. You didn't say much about it."

"There isn't much to tell." Solier shrugged again. "He died from a sunstroke. As I said, Mark Arnhardt brought his body back to Amarillo."

"His interest in the place, you say, passed to Arnhardt?"

"Yes."

Rennert watched the smoke rise from his cigar.

"I used to be an addict of western yarns," he said with a faint smile. "If I remember right, there was always a band of rival cattlemen trying to get control of the ranch that the hero worked for. Is it possible that this is true in this case?"

"You're thinking about the difficulty with the water?"

"Yes."

Solier laughed drily.

"Not a chance. Wait until you see the country and you'll agree with me. There's not another building, except an occasional adobe Indian hut, for fifty miles. If anybody was fool enough to want to get a ranch in that section of the country there's all the land he wants, almost for the asking."

"But you said your company had to pay the Flores family a big price for their land?"

Solier hesitated.

"Yes, that's true, but it was a good location and they got wind of the reason we wanted it and held us up. I admit that to you, privately."

"No mineral deposits?"

"None that I know of. The land's useless without irrigation. You might as well save your energies as far as that angle is concerned." Solier's eyes fell, rested for an instant on the check, then rose again. "Will you take the job, Rennert?"

Rennert took a last contemplative draw upon his cigar.

"Yes," he said.

"Good!" Solier sat up in his chair. His nervousness seemed to vanish, to be replaced by brisk efficiency. "When can you start?"

"As soon as the matter is arranged at Washington."

Solier waved this aside.

"I'll wire Senator Jenkins at once. He'll fix it up. You ought to be able to leave tomorrow."

"Very well."

"Now as to details," he tapped the little finger of his left hand against the edge of the desk. "Some minor matters first. There are a few things I want to send down with you and then there are Miss Fahn's postcards that we mustn't forget."

His eyes met Rennert's. He smiled.

"You see, you're beginning to run into the old girl's peculiarities already. Falter says she wants some postcards. I wish you'd get them for her. One hundred and twenty-six."

"One hundred and twenty-six? She specified the exact number?"

"Yes."

"But what kind of cards?"

"Oh, any kind, just so they're postcards. Get her some pictures of the Alamo and the Missions and that sort of stuff. Then—"

"But just a minute," Rennert interrupted. "She didn't specify any particular views?"

"No, she just wants postcards. Going to send them to all the folks back in Austin, I suppose. Now, as to communication. I told you there was a short-wave radio set at the hacienda. I have another at my home." He took a pencil from his pocket and drew a memorandum pad toward him. "My station is W10XAKI," he traced the name carefully upon the paper, "10.22 megacycles. The station at the hacienda—it's licensed by the Mexican Government, of course—is XADY. Hours on the air from 6 to 7 A.M. and P.M. You might arrange to stand by your set during those hours. I'll do the same or arrange to have any messages of yours telephoned to me in case I'm at the office. Satisfactory?"

Solier tore the slip from the pad and handed it to Rennert.

"That's number three. Now," his index finger was beating a tattoo against the wood, "as to the location of the hacienda. You have a car?"

Rennert nodded.

"You'll drive down, I suppose?"

"Yes, I'd prefer to drive myself."

"Good!" Solier got to his feet and walked across the room to the wall on the left, where hung a large map of the Mexican republic.

Rennert followed him.

Solier ran a finger southward from San Antonio, across the Rio Grande at Laredo.

"You follow the Pan-American Highway through Monterrey to Hidalgo. Turn off to the right there in the direction of Aramberri...."

2
ENCOUNTER IN THE SUN

THE SUN HAD dislodged itself from the zenith, where it had stuck motionless and staring for seemingly interminable hours, and was moving at last toward the west. Its rays shot in under the projecting eaves of the roof and limned Ann Tolman's loose mass of hair in bright copper.

She leaned wearily against one of the square wooden posts that supported the roof and let her hands rest against her thighs. The heavy odors of the sun-baked earth of the patio and of the flowers with which it was filled were almost stifling. She stared upward, over the flowers and the dry fountain and the red-tiled roof, into the vastness of the gray-brown Mountains and hot blue sky.

She was thinking, lethargically, of that lush northern spring when she and Stephen, drunk with the air and fragile dreams and pounding young blood, had married. It had been Commencement week, a Carnival of loosened emotions and foolishly inflated ambitions. They had driven into the night, after a fraternity dance, and had aroused the justice of the peace of some little village, the name of which she couldn't recall now.

She brushed a hand across her eyes. Incredibly remote, it all seemed, unassociated with reality.

The serrated tops of the mountains wavered, as if they had given off a suddenly intensified radiation of heat waves.

She was too tired now to protest any longer against the remorselessness with which things had tumbled about their heads. The families of neither had been in a position to aid them. Modest investments had been swept away in the cataclysm of the depression. There had been no demand for architects, even good ones as (she told herself again loyally) Stephen undoubtedly was. And then the final numbing blow. Tuberculosis, the doctors had pronounced it. Stephen must have rest in another and drier climate. There had been talk of sanitariums, frantic plans that flooded vainly against the granite wall of impecunity. They had moved to Texas, where Stephen had found a job. They had gotten along fairly well for a time. Then had come that incredible incident in San Antonio, the thought of which sent hot tears of resentment to her young eyes and contracted the fingers of her hands into tight little fists.

She had known then the fierce white flame that makes people kill.

She let her eyes fall and stared at the yellow marigolds at her feet. A mass of them occupied the entire corner of the patio in which she stood. Their heads were drooping toward the hard, dark soil that had cracked crazily in little zigzags.

She had endured these two months of heat and loneliness because the climate was helping Stephen. But now they said that the rains were about to commence, that day after day throughout the summer there would be showers—the fierce pounding showers of the tropics. Stephen must be gotten out before they came. . . .

She saw it, lying very still and wary, coiled under a dense clump of the marigolds. Two black flakes of light regarded her with lidless fixity. As she stared, fascinated by a coldness that the eyes clamped about her heart, she heard a tiny sound. It was harsh and rasping, like two stiff withered leaves vibrating against each other.

She started to draw back then stopped, the fingers of one hand tight about the post.

Here was a way. It would neither be quick nor painless—but no one would ever suspect.

The rasping filled her ears. The sound steeled her with determination, breaking the tension that gripped her as she stared at those two steady eyes.

If I could only tell Steve, she thought. A queer distorted little prayer flitted across her mind.

She moved forward. . . .

"*Hacienda Flores*," Rennert read with dust-weary eyes.

The letters had been burned deep into a huge hewn beam, the ends of which rested upon the tops of two stone pillars.

He drew a handkerchief from his pocket and passed it across his face. In his ears was the gentle churning of the water in the radiator, heated by hours of driving over uneven roads.

He looked about him, paying silent tribute to the wild beauty of the setting.

Straight ahead of him rose the mountains, barren gray-brown slopes that shot suddenly up into sheer walls of rock, above and beyond which rose higher peaks, their outlines lost in a thin haze of heat. Against the horizon, as he narrowed his eyes, he could distinguish the shimmering blue shapes of farther, mirage-like ranges.

The hacienda lay in a pocket of the mountains, where a precipitous valley debouched onto the desert. Its adobe walls had evidently once been painted a bright vermilion, traces of which remained obstinately in irregular splotches on the gray surface. A wide, open doorway and two narrow barred windows broke the monotony of the front. From the sloping tiled roof projected the ends of round logs, like cannon aimed at an intruder.

It was a building as characteristic of the Mexican landscape as the mountains and the mesquite and the cruel claws of the maguey. One had the feeling that it, too, had grown out of the soil.

Two objects jarred with their blatant notes of modernity. On the slope to the left of the house stood a square one-story building of red brick. Nearer at hand, half hidden by the corner of the adobe walls, was a small biplane, its wings bright silver in the sun.

Rennert started the car and drove straight ahead, under the rude archway. He came to a stop at one side of the entrance and got out, shaking loose the clothing that clung damply to his body. His muscles ached from the hours spent in the jolting car. He longed to plunge into cold clear water, to cleanse body and brain.

A suitcase in either hand he walked toward the doorway. It was so wide that he might easily have driven the car through it. His feet, crunching against the loose gravel, sounded unnaturally loud in the heavy afternoon stillness that held the place.

He stopped in the entrance, staring in surprise at the interior. He felt as if he had stepped into a greenhouse.

The patio, around which the house was built, was larger than he had expected from his survey of the exterior. A tiled fountain rose out of a stone basin. Beyond this he caught a glimpse of another inner patio. Both were filled (confusingly, was his first impression) with flowers.

However, as he advanced, he saw that there was a certain symmetrical arrangement about them.

The stone base of the fountain was hidden by a bed of flaming red poinsettias. In a narrow circle about these was a variety of poppy with white crêpe-like petals. In the far corners were a frangipani tree, its flowers white and gold against long glistening green leaves, and a mass of white-trumpeted floripondio blossoms.

He stepped inside.

Between the fioripondios and the corner at his left were regular beds of flowers whose names he did not know, with clover-like heads of white and red and violet. The corner itself was filled with tiny *flores del Indio*, cardinal red. Straight in front of him was a star-shaped bed of gentian-blue gilias. To his right a dazzling-bright profusion of yellow marigolds.

A girl in a plain faded blue dress was standing a few feet from the marigolds, by the wooden post that supported the roof. She was staring fixedly at the ground. As Rennert watched she began to move forward, walking with stiff mechanical steps.

Rennert moved into the shade and advanced toward her. She didn't seem to hear his footsteps on the worn flagstones.

He got within a few feet of her and stopped, puzzled by her actions.

His ears caught the note of warning. The rasping was loud now, grating angrily into the hot silence.

He looked down and saw the brown quivering coil under the marigolds.

He sprang forward, caught her by the shoulders and pushed her back. He stepped quickly to one side and jerked loose a stone from the paving. He threw it just as the brown coil unwound.

A thud and the long loose end of the coil writhed frantically, filling the air with its buzzing rattle.

"For God's sake, woman—" He turned to the girl and stopped.

She was standing by the post, one bare arm encircling it. The other hung straight down at her side. She was staring at the ground, her light brown eyes widened by horror. The white skin seemed suddenly stretched tightly over the bones of her small delicately chiseled face. Her chin was firm but the bloodless lips above it were tightly compressed, as if to quiet the tendon that quivered spasmodically in her bare throat.

She raised her eyes very slowly and looked at him dazedly.

She said in a flat, tired voice: "You might have saved yourself the trouble, you know. There are so many ways."

3
A BLOW

THE GIRL STARTED across the patio, along a graveled path that ran between rectangular beds of red coral-bells and lilac zinnias. A few steps and she stopped, her shoulders sagging.

Rennert went to her side and put an arm about her. She steadied herself, her head thrown back so that the sun shone full on it. He observed the dark circles below her averted eyes, the telltale lines that had etched her thin cheeks.

"I'm all right," she spoke with a visible effort. "I'm going to my room."

"Let me help you."

She made no reply but accompanied him, the fingers of one hand grasping his sleeve tightly. He felt the uncontrollable trembling of her arm.

As they came to a door on the west side she stopped, looked up at his face and said in a low voice, little more than a whisper: "There's no need to say anything, is there?"

"About the snake?"

"About what I was going to do."

"None at all."

"Thanks." She put out a hand and opened the door. She paused on the threshold.

A tall young man clad in white pajamas was advancing out of the dim coolness of the room. He came forward and threw an arm about the girl.

"Ann! What's the matter?"

A little tremor ran through her body and she buried her head against his shoulder, one hand running up the side of his temple to bury itself in his ruffled yellow hair.

"It was a rattlesnake," Rennert explained. "She came very near stepping on it."

"Oh!" He saw the quick flare of concern in the light blue eyes that were rimmed by dark shadows. The man's face was long and handsome but weakened by an indeterminate chin. He stared at Rennert for a moment then extended a hand. "Tolman's my name. This is my wife, Ann."

"My name is Rennert. I'm to be a guest here at the hacienda for a while."

He felt the soft thin-boned hand press ineffectually against his large tanned one before they released their grip.

"Thank you, Rennert," Tolman said. He looked straight into Rennert's eyes and repeated: "Thank you," as if he were impressing upon him some special message.

"Could you tell me," Rennert asked, "where I can find Mr. Falter?"

"That's his room over there on the north side, to the right of the entrance to the inside patio."

"Much obliged. And now," Rennert had been observing the girl's face, "I think it would be well if Mrs. Tolman lay down for a while. She had quite a shock."

"Oh, yes, of course." Her husband was quickly apologetic.

They turned into the room and closed the door.

Rennert stared for a moment, thoughtfully, at the thick wooden panels before he walked away.

He knocked at the door that Tolman had indicated.

It was thrown open almost immediately by a florid, heavy-featured man with sparse, sandy-colored hair. A faded olive-colored shirt and gray drill trousers hung loosely upon a frame that would have been capable of supporting a great deal of solid flesh and muscle. He looked sixty and might have been forty.

"Mr. Falter?" Rennert inquired.

"Yes, you're Rennert?" The voice was deep and heavy with a suggestion of Germanic gutturalness. "I had a talk with Ed Solier this morning and he said you were on your way down. Glad to see you."

He gripped Rennert's hand and looked straight and appraisingly into his eyes. His own hard china-blue eyes were sun-narrowed. He blinked them as if he had been aroused from sleep.

"Come in," he said, "or would you rather get washed up first?"

"I'd like to get at least one layer of this dust off, if you don't mind."

"I expect so. I'll show you where your room is. Where are your things?"

"Over by the door."

Rennert followed him along the narrow stone-paved path that circled the patio under the shelter of the roof.

"Have a good trip down?" Falter asked conversationally.

"Hot and dry and dusty, but it's what I expected."

"You've been in this part of Mexico before, I believe?"

"Yes, I've spent a considerable number of years along the border."

They retrieved Rennert's suitcases and carried them to a door on the east side. Falter gestured toward it.

"Here you are. I expect you'll want a bath?"

"It's almost a necessity in my present condition."

"All right. I had Miguel fill up a tub this afternoon. It runs pretty slow and I thought you wouldn't want to wait. You'll find the bathroom in the inside patio. If there's anything you want, just shout."

Rennert had opened the door and was already peeling off a coat that had once been white.

"You'll have to pardon a little confusion around here," Falter was glancing about him. "Miguel, the Mexican who acts as a sort of manager of the place, was taken sick a couple of hours ago. He didn't have time to get all the things moved out of this room."

"This looks very comfortable. Is the man seriously ill?"

"Oh, no, I don't think so." Falter went to the door, turned back and said: "Come on into my room when you get through and we'll have a drink."

As he loosened his tie Rennert looked about him. The floor of the room was of dark red tiles, upon which lay a heavy blue-and-gray sarape. Overhead, huge beams had been patinated by time to metal smoothness. The walls were calcimined a light blue, restful to eyes that had to endure the glare of the sun outside. There was a bed with clean white sheets, an enormous wardrobe with mirrors set in the panels of its doors, a washstand and two chairs. Beneath the deep barred window stood a small metal trunk, bearing the initials EOS. Evidently a relic of Solier's visit to the hacienda.

Rennert relaxed in the coolness and began to burrow in his luggage for clean clothing.

Half an hour later he stood before one of the mirrors, straightening his tie. There was a slight frown on his wide tanned forehead and the eyes that followed the movements of his fingers were thoughtful. His mind was on that scene in the patio, the snake coiled under the flowers and the white-faced girl who had walked through the sun toward it. If there had been any doubt about her intentions her words had effectually dispelled it. Did her husband suspect what she had been about to do? There had been, unless he was mistaken, a queer troubled look deep down in the blue eyes that had looked into his. Yet there had been no mistaking the manner in which the girl's head had sought his shoulder, the gentle protectiveness of his arm as it went around her body.

He went to the bed and picked up the soiled suit that he had worn to the hacienda. He carried it to the wardrobe, opened one of the doors and hung it upon a hook. There was a shelf just above and on the shelf an empty Habanero whisky bottle.

Dazzling bright sunlight flooded into the room. He turned.

A young man was standing with one hand on the knob of the door and staring at him. As Rennert's eyes accustomed themselves to the glare he had an impression of a well-built, compactly muscled body clad in baggy seersucker trousers and a flannel shirt. The shirt splayed open at the top to reveal a brown stocky throat. The shoulders were broad and straight.

The newcomer strode into the room, moving easily with a lithe swinging gait.

"Hello!" he said, a bit awkwardly. "Sorry I bothered you. I'm Mark Arnhardt. I suppose you're Mr. Rennert?"

"Yes."

They shook hands perfunctorily.

Glancing at Arnhardt's face one would have noticed his eyes first. They were clear dark brown and the pupils seemed to protrude slightly, like two very bright marbles. They gave the effect of a bold disconcerting stare. Looking more closely, one saw that there was something gentle and friendly about their directness that offset the superficial sternness of his strong plainly featured countenance.

"Glad to have you with us, Mr. Rennert." He hesitated. "I suppose I ought to explain why I came busting in here like I did. I didn't know you were in here, you see. I thought it was still my own room." He looked about him. "Falter must have moved my stuff while I was out this afternoon."

"See here," Rennert protested, "I don't want to disturb you. I can take another room."

"Oh, no, it doesn't matter," the other said quickly. "This is cooler and you aren't as used to the heat as we are." He hooked his right thumb about his belt and let his shoulders sag forward. He stood for a moment, planted in this posture of well-balanced relaxation, and seemed to be trying to think of something further to say.

"Going to be with us long?" he asked.

"Several days, at any rate."

"Well," Arnhardt swung around, "I've got to go and find out where Falter moved me to." He unloosened his thumb and thrust his hand into a trousers pocket. "Glad to have met you, Mr. Rennert. See you later." His smile was pleasant as he closed the door.

Rennert felt in his pocket for cigarettes. He felt a mental alertness, the result of several factors: the cool water which had splashed his tired body, the confrontation with a problem which had its origin in the tap roots of some individual's behavior and (although be would not have admitted it verbally) the insistent presence about him of the hot enigmatic sensuousness of Mexico.

As he walked into the patio and strolled toward Falter's room he heard a low murmur of conversation coming from the open door.

He stopped to light his cigarette under the frangipani tree that rose above him to a height of at least twenty feet, charging the air with the sweet cloying odor of its white golden-hearted blossoms.

The murmur fused into a strong young voice raised in anger—
the same voice that Rennert had heard a few moments earlier in
his own room. Its hesitancy was gone now.

"I'll have you remember that I'm as much an owner of this ranch
and this house as you are. I've got as much to say about the living
arrangements as you have. You haven't any right to move me about
from room to room without consulting me. Understand?"

There was a low rumble of protest from Falter. "I told you when
you moved in there that that room was Solier's, that he didn't want
anyone in there. He told me to put Rennert there and I did. If you've
got any kick register it with him, not with me."

Arnhardt's voice cut in: "To hell with Solier! He can't lock up a
room on the east side of the house and expect it to stay vacant until he gets ready to come back."

"Well, run the Tolmans out of their room if you want to. They—"

"Yes, and that reminds me of another thing I've been wanting
to tell you for a long time." Arnhardt raised his voice still higher.
"It's about the Tolmans. Ann told me about the damned dirty deal
they've gotten from you and Solier. I'm going to see that you two
get paid back for that if it's the last thing I do. I won't—"

The door of a room across the patio opened and a young Mexican came out. He wore boots, corduroy trousers and a khaki shirt.
A broad-brimmed straw hat shaded a finely featured face across
which a thin waxed mustache looked like a painted line. He carried a square case of black leather and a spade. He regarded
Rennert for a moment with a steady direct stare then, with no sign
of greeting, walked toward the entrance.

As Rennert's eyes followed him he reminded himself that eaves-
dropping is not judged as harshly in Mexico as among Anglo-Sax-
ons.

"You young fool!" Falter's voice was hoarse and guttural. "If
anything happened to the Tolmans your stepfather, George Stahl,
was responsible as much as Solier and I. You've let yourself be
taken in by hard-luck stories from that red-headed—"

A fist cracked smartly against flesh. A splintering crash was
the echo.

4
DAMP EARTH

MARK ARNHARDT'S FEET struck the paving like pistons as he came out of the room and headed straight across the patio. His fists were clenched tightly at his sides and his chin was thrust forward belligerently. If he saw Rennert he made no indication of it but entered a room to the left of the entrance and slammed the door behind him.

Rennert stood in the shade by the frangipani tree and flicked ash from his cigarette. His eyes followed it to the ground and he frowned.

About the base of the tree was a bed of Oliver's flowers, thrusting out blood-red stars tipped with yellow from spatulate green and crimson leaves. Between them and the paving where he stood was an expanse of bare soil, broken into irregular blocks by a network of cracks.

He stepped forward and kicked the ground with the toe of his shoe. The hard surface resisted at first. He pressed his weight against his foot, the baked upper layer broke and his shoe plowed into loose darker earth. He knelt down and took a bit of it between his fingers.

It was damp.

He straightened up and let the soil fall slowly from his hand. He stood for a moment, his face thoughtful, then walked toward the open door of Falter's quarters. He tapped against the side.

There was a moment of silence then a voice called gruffly from inside: "Come in."

Rennert entered a small square room furnished with a large desk, scarred by usage, and a swivel chair. A straight chair to one side of the desk had been overturned. One of the rungs at the back was broken. Several dusty calendars advertising various brands of beer adorned the blue-tinted walls. It served, evidently, as office for the master of the hacienda.

Falter came out of the adjoining room. His face was flushed and he held a handkerchief to the side of his mouth.

"Oh, hello, Rennert." He spoke indistinctly through the folds of the cloth. "Sit down." He gestured toward a chair on the other side of the desk and, as Rennert moved toward it, he hastily straightened the overturned chair.

"Hot, isn't it?" He pulled open a drawer of the desk and brought out a bottle of Habanero and two glasses. "We've got some beer, if you'd rather have it." He spoke jerkily, out of one side of his mouth.

"This whisky will do, thanks."

Falter went to the door and called: "Maria!"

There was no response.

He called again.

"*Si, señor,*" came a woman's answering voice, evidently from the inner patio.

"*Tráenos agua.*"

"*Bueno.*"

Falter came back and sat down behind the desk, crossing his legs. He kept the handkerchief pressed against his face.

"Get settled all right?" he asked.

"Yes, the bath put a brighter aspect on things. I'm sure I'll be very comfortable. I just wondered, however, if I hadn't inconvenienced someone."

"How's that?" Falter's eyes came quickly to his face.

"The room you put me in is on the east side, I notice. It must be one of the choice ones. Young Arnhardt had it, I understand. I could have taken another."

Falter patted his mouth gently with the handkerchief.

"That's all right." He stared past Rennert's head. "It's really Solier's room. He used it when he was here. He told me to put you in it. Arnhardt can take another just as well as not."

There was a moment of silence.

"How's the weather been up in Texas?" Falter asked abstractedly.

"Much the same as here—hot and dry. It's what we expect, however. You usually have rains down here by this time."

"Yes, so they say. They've been unusually late in starting. It has been the worst spring I ever went through."

He glanced at the door.

A thin Mexican woman entered. Her shoulders were bent as if from long support of burdens. Her face, moulded in the high-checked features of the pure Mexican aborigine, was like wrinkled parchment. Her long glistening hair, black, shot through with gray, hung in two symmetrical braids. In one hand she carried a clay jug beaded with moisture, in the other a bunch of red hibiscus flowers.

She set the jug on the desk and turned to go.

"Maria," Falter said, "*éste es el señor Rennert, que está de visita aquí.*"

She turned vague black eyes, with a distinct mongoloid cast, on Rennert's face.

"*Mucho gusto, señor.*" Her voice was soft but to Rennert, accustomed to the staccato birdlike voices of Mexican women, it sounded singularly flat and expressionless.

"*El gusto es mío,*" he spoke in reply to her salutation.

"Oh," Falter seemed surprised, "you speak Spanish."

"Yes, I get along fairly well with it."

"*Cómo está Miguel?*" Falter asked Maria.

For an instant some emotion seemed about to break the mask of her face. It betrayed itself in the almost imperceptible trembling of her thin lips, in the febrile brightness that glinted across the dark surfaces of her eyes and was gone.

"*Muy malo, señor, muy malo,*" she said tonelessly.

Falter frowned. "I'll send in to Victoria for a doctor," he said in Spanish.

She shook her head vigorously and her fingers tightened about the stems of the red flowers.

"No, señor! No, señor! Do not do it! If he is cured, I must do it."

"But, Maria," Falter said patiently, "a doctor would know better than you what to do. You don't even know what's the matter with Miguel."

Her voice too was patient: "Yes, señor, I know. I know."

"What is it?"

Her eyes went to the top of the desk, wandered for an instant over its surface, then focused on the jug of water.

"It is nothing, señor, nothing but a little illness," she seemed to be speaking to herself—or, the odd thought struck Rennert, *to the water itself.* "It will go."

"Very well," Falter's tone was nettled, "just as you say. Let me know, though, if you want a doctor."

"*Muy bien, señor, gracias.*"

The woman turned toward the door, hesitated, then faced them again. She held out the hibiscus flowers.

"These flowers," she spoke quickly, "they are red, are they not, señor?"

Falter had extended his hand toward the whisky bottle. He let it fall to the desk and stared at her.

"What?"

"These flowers," there was quiet persistence in her manner, "they are red, are they not?"

"Of course. What color did you think they were?"

She turned to Rennert.

"You, too, señor, you see that they are red?" A faint suggestion of eagerness tinged her voice.

Rennert had leaned forward to watch her more closely. The cigarette burned unheeded in his fingers.

"Yes," he said quietly, "they are red."

She turned again to Falter. Her breathing was more rapid now, her breast rising and falling perceptibly under the dark blue *rebozo* which she wore.

"You will tell him, señor? You will tell Miguel?"

"Tell him what?" Falter's voice and face expressed his bewilderment.

"That these flowers are red. They," she stole a cautious sideways glance at the water jug, "are playing tricks with him. This afternoon, when he fell sick, there were white *claveles* in the room. Pure white. I picked them this morning. He thought that they were yellow. I take him now these red flowers so that he will know there are no yellow flowers in his room."

Rennert had not taken his eyes from her face.

"Did Miguel," he asked, "have fear when he saw—or thought he saw—the yellow flowers?"

She regarded him for a long moment, then her head moved slowly up and down in affirmation.

"Yes, he had much fear." She turned, murmured. "*Hasta luego, señores*," and left them.

"What the hell?" Falter laughed uncertainly as he stared after her into the sunlight.

5
YELLOW FLOWERS

FALTER POURED WHISKY into the glasses. He shoved two tumblers forward and filled them with water from the jug. Some of the liquid splashed over the desk-top.

"Have a drink," he said with forced joviality as he handed Rennert a glass.

Rennert brought his attention back to the room. He had been staring, since Maria left, out the window, where transverse bars of iron divided the view of a bed of white carnations in the inner patio. In response to a gesture from Falter he raised his glass and drank.

"I suppose I ought to have told you something about Maria," Falter was saying as he set down his glass. He ran the tip of his tongue over his upper lip. "She's a little loose up here," he pointed to his fore head. "They say she had some bad experiences during the Revolution, when a bunch of bandits captured the hacienda. She's harmless, of course. Spends most of her time pottering about among the flowers. I don't know what was on her mind just now. She must be worrying too much about Miguel."

"What about Miguel's illness? You say he was taken sick this afternoon?"

"Yes, a couple of hours or so before you came. I'd told him to move Arnhardt's stuff out of that room. He worked there a while then Maria came in to tell me that he was sick and couldn't do any more."

"You haven't seen him?"

"I went in his room a little later—they live back in the inside patio—and tried to find out what the trouble was. He was lying on the bed and wouldn't talk. He seemed to be suffering but I didn't know what to do. Maria came back in a few minutes with a bunch of herbs that she'd gathered out in the mountains. Evidently she was going to brew some kind of concoction out of them. They're superstitious as hell, these Mexicans, and don't trust doctors from the cities. If he doesn't get better tonight I'll send for a doctor anyway, regardless of what the old woman says. Miguel is invaluable around here."

Falter leaned forward and took up his glass. He glanced inquiringly at Rennert, who shook his head. He filled his own glass brimful and tossed it down his throat.

"God!" he took a deep breath of satisfaction. "I needed that." He looked at Rennert for a moment, frankly appraising him. "Rennert," he said, his voice suddenly unconstrained, "you bring me thoughts of cold white milk and ice and toasted wheat bread and hard yellow slabs of butter—things one almost forgets about down here."

Rennert smiled. "Really, I didn't know that I portrayed so nicely the solid puritan virtues. I'm afraid it's only middle age and the fact that I've just had a bath for the first time in two days."

Falter's smile was ineffectual. "No, it's not that at all. It's the state of health I've been in lately. Tortillas and beans aren't meant for a white man's diet. Maria is a good enough cook in her way but her menu is limited. We had a Chinese cook up until a few weeks ago but he left us, saved up enough money to go visit some friends in Mexico City. I've been hoping he'd come back soon. By the way, did Solier send some tablets down by you?"

"Yes, I have them here." Rennert took out a box which Solier had given him in San Antonio and laid it on the table.

"Good!" Falter took it eagerly. "I've been wanting some more of those. They may save my stomach until Lee gets back. They're the best cure for indigestion I know of," he explained as he opened the box and took out a white wafer. He swallowed it and took a drink of water. "How is Solier?" he asked.

"Seems to be all right. He's been rather busy and wants to get away for a vacation. That's the reason he didn't come down himself."

Falter sat for a moment with a frown of concentration on his face. He looked up suddenly and met Rennert's gaze.

"Just what," he asked, "did Solier tell you about things down here?"

"He told me of the plan to build a hotel that had to be abandoned on account of the change in the route of the highway. He told me about Miss Fahn's refusal to sell her shares and about the disappearance of the water. He wanted me to persuade Miss Fahn to sell, if possible, and to learn who was responsible for the theft of the water. I am to offer the woman the full price she paid for the shares, if necessary."

Falter's short stubby fingers were caressing the sides of the glass. He kept nodding his head as Rennert spoke.

"I'm glad you came," he said slowly, "although I'm not sure you can do any good. Miss Fahn's a tough proposition. I've got the feeling that it's not a question of money with her so much as something else. What, I don't know."

In his preoccupation Falter took the handkerchief from his mouth. On the right side there was an ugly discolored bruise, from which blood still welled.

"Can you tell me something about her?" Rennert asked. "Give me some pointers on how to approach her?"

"God, no!" Falter shook his head decidedly. "I don't think she is approachable. Unless," he eyed Rennert speculatively, "you happen to be a religious man. She's very much that way, objects to profanity, drinking, gambling," he paused for a fractional second, "and all that sort of thing."

Rennert smiled. "I'll have to restrain my appetites, then."

"You certainly will if you want to get along with her. Of course if you know anything about plants and flowers, that might make up for other shortcomings."

"I understood that she was a botanist."

"Yes, she spends all her time tramping around the hills gathering flowers and leaves and things. By the way, did you bring those postcards she wanted?"

"Yes, one hundred and twenty-six of them. That the right number?"

"Yes, she's been pestering me for a week to have Solier send some down."

"She must carry on a lot of correspondence?"

Falter shook his head. "No, that's the strange thing about her wanting them. She hasn't gotten any mail or sent any off since she's been here."

"You're sure?" Rennert was interested.

"Yes, Miguel goes in to Victoria twice a week. He always brings all the mail to me when he gets back. There's never anything for Miss Fahn. I asked him if he ever took any in for her and he said he didn't."

"Frankly," Rennert said, "I'm getting rather curious to meet Miss Fahn. Now, as to the disappearance of the water, do you have any information to give me?"

"Not a thing. It's got me puzzled. Every night lately a five-gallon glass bottle of water has vanished. The bottle itself is always in place in the morning but the water is gone."

"Where is the water kept?"

"In the kitchen, in the inner patio."

"It's locked at night?"

"Yes."

"The obvious question: How many people have keys?"

"Maria and I had one apiece. She lost hers several weeks ago and has had to use mine since. I lock up myself at night when she has finished and unlock in the morning. Yet somebody gets in every night. No one person could drink that much water, however."

"Solier said that you thought someone might be trying to force the occupants of the hacienda to leave."

"Yes," Falter pressed the handkerchief more firmly against his mouth, "the thought had occurred to me that that might be the explanation. Who it could be, though, I don't have any idea."

"I noticed," Rennert said, "that the soil out in the patio has been well watered recently. There are the cracks that the sun makes on damp ground. Underneath, there is dampness. I should say," he looked keenly at Falter, "that water was poured there not later than last night."

"And last night," Falter's face held frank astonishment, "another bottle of water was emptied."

"Those flowers, too, look as if they had plenty of moisture. Are they watered regularly?"

"No, they haven't been for several weeks. Maria takes care of them but I told her to quit watering them when the fountain out there went dry."

There was silence for a moment.

"There's one more matter I'd like to bring up," Rennert said. "It's about George Stahl's death."

Falter's thick eyebrows drew together swiftly. "What do you mean?" he demanded.

"I'd like to have all the particulars that you can recall."

"Did Solier ask you to inquire into that?" Falter's voice was perceptibly edged.

"Not precisely." Rennert's manner was almost casual. "His instructions were to look into everything of an unusual nature that has happened about here lately. I thought that Stahl's death would naturally, come under that category."

"I don't see how. He died of a sunstroke."

"Suppose you tell me about it."

"Good God! There's nothing more to tell!" Falter broke out in open impatience. "It was early in the afternoon, during the siesta, when the sun is at its hottest. Stahl wasn't used to it and went out in the patio without a hat on. He was found there, where he had fallen."

"Who found him?"

"His stepson, Mark Arnhardt."

"How soon after that did he die?"

"A little after midnight that night."

"Was he conscious any of the time?"

"Yes, I suppose you'd call it conscious. He acted sort of dazed and afraid and was in a lot of pain—in the stomach and abdomen, it seemed. I think the sun affected his brain. For a long time he kept talking about how yellow the air was."

Rennert said sharply: "Yellow?"

"Yes." Falter reached over, filled another glass with water and drank it. "Several times while I was in the room with him he mentioned it."

"Was anyone with him before he died?"

"Yes, Arnhardt and Ann Tolman took turns staying by his bed."

Rennert leaned forward to tap ashes into a brown earthenware bowl. His face was grave.

"Were there any flowers in his room?" he asked.

"Flowers? Why, I don't remember."

"In what part of the patio," Rennert persisted, "was Stahl lying when he was found?"

"On the south side, the corner between the main door and your room."

"Near the bed of yellow marigolds?"

"Yes. In fact, I believe he had actually fallen into the marigolds." Falter continued to look at him speculatively. "What's the matter?" There was a tight strained quality to his voice. "What have those flowers got to do with it?"

Rennert didn't answer for a moment. He raised the cigarette to his lips and inhaled slowly. He let the smoke trickle through his nostrils and said: "Nothing, probably. But don't you see the coincidence?"

Falter stared at him. There were little beads of perspiration standing out on his forehead.

"You mean with Miguel's talk about the flowers being yellow?" He spoke as if unwillingly.

"Yes—and with that particular color of flower."

"What do you mean?"

"Don't you know what yellow flowers—specifically yellow marigolds—mean throughout the length and breadth of Mexico?"

"No, I can't say that I do."

"They mean," Rennert said quietly, "death."

6
MOIST FINGERS ON GLASS

FALTER SAT UPRIGHT in his chair, his hands gripping the edge of the desk. The handkerchief lay unheeded before him.

"Oh, see here!" he protested. "That's being rather melodramatic, isn't it?"

Rennert nodded. "Very. I merely remarked on the coincidence."

The light glinted against Falter's narrowed blue eyes. His voice was faintly derisive: "Yet you put some stock in it," he stated rather than asked.

"At least," Rennert said evenly, "I don't deny the possibility that there's some factor there I haven't grasped yet. Things have a way of happening in a melodramatic manner in Mexico."

Neither of them spoke for several seconds.

Rennert felt a thin trickle of perspiration run down his cheek. His clothing adhered to his body. The exhilaration which had followed his bath was gone now and in its place he was conscious of a sensation of lassitude, as if the air in the room were growing stale and oppressively heavy. He realized that he was breathing with his mouth partially open. He glanced into the patio, half-shadowed by the slanting rays of the sun, and wondered when the coolness that comes with sunset on the desert would begin to make itself felt. . . .

The doorway was vacant one moment. The next moment a figure stood there, silhouetted against the light.

"Lee! I'll be damned!" Falter cried. He got to his feet and strode around the side of the desk as a little wizened Chinaman came into the room.

The man wore a baggy blue serge suit and, incongruously, a tight slipover sweater of robin's-egg blue. He was nodding vigorously, a broad smile rounding his face.

"Hello, boss! Glad see you again."

Falter went up and clapped a hand on his shoulder.

"Glad to see *you*, Lee. Where in the hell have you been?"

Lee's black button-like eyes twinkled with inner merriment.

"Mexico City, boss. Have good time, see uncle and cousins. Money all gone now. Come back cook."

"Fine. The kitchen's yours. What about a good dinner tonight, like you used to cook?"

"Good dinner, good dinner, yes. Velly soon now." Lee nodded his small sparsely covered head.

"There are seven of us now, Lee. Mr. Rennert here is staying with us."

The Chinaman jerked his head toward Rennert and, after a moment's scrutiny, said with no alteration of his smile: "Velly glad to know, boss."

When he had gone Rennert said to Falter: "Suppose we take this opportunity to look at the kitchen ourselves."

"All right."

Outside Falter stopped for a moment at the edge of the paving and thrust a toe into the ground.

"You're right," he nodded without looking at Rennert, "water *has* been spilled out here. Lots of it, too."

They entered the inner patio through an arch, over which climbed a many-tendriled vine alive with a species of russet and maroon orchid.

The patio itself was similar to the outer one, but smaller and without a fountain. Rennert, glancing hastily over the flowers with which it was filled, caught the red of hibiscus and the golden yellow of marigolds. He said to Falter: "I can't get over my surprise at these flowers. If this were in New York a florist would have a fortune here."

Falter said without much interest: "Yes, I suppose it is unusual to find so many kinds growing in this part of the country. I understand that in the old days the Flores family went in for flowers in a big way, brought specimens here from all over Mexico. Being right on the Tropic of Cancer they could cultivate both tropical and temperate varieties. I understand that Toledano Flores—that was the grandfather of the young Mexican who's staying here—did a lot of experimenting and produced some new varieties. Lots of them died during the Revolution but Maria has kept most of them alive."

"'Flores' means 'flowers.' I suppose these gardens were a sort of family monument, as it were."

"I suppose so." Falter turned to the left and led the way to a room on the west.

It was a large square room, paved with worn dark red tiles. The ceiling was darkened by smoke. A tiled charcoal stove stood opposite the door. Polished pans and other utensils hung about the walls.

Lee stood in the center, his gaze darting quickly from object to object, as if taking inventory.

Maria Montemayor was in the corner, bending over a steaming pottery bowl that rested on a flat circular tray of clay set on a horseshoe-shaped hearth of plastered stones. She looked up as they entered but said nothing. Rennert noticed that she kept her eyes carefully averted from the Chinaman.

Lee gestured with a thumb toward the adjoining room.

"Have all same room, boss?" he inquired.

"Yes," Falter told him, "you can have the same room. Nobody's used it since you left."

Rennert had walked over to the south wall and was kneeling upon the floor, where stood five glass bottles. One of them was empty, another partially so. He gestured toward the empty one.

"This was emptied last night?"

"Yes." Falter came and stood beside him.

Rennert stared at it thoughtfully for a moment.

"Do you mind," he asked, getting up, "if I take it to my room?"

"Sure not." Falter's perpetually narrowed eyes fastened on Rennert's face. "Fingerprints?" he asked in a low voice.

Rennert had taken out his handkerchief and with it picked up the bottle.

"Yes, unless I'm mistaken there are some on this glass."

"I thought about looking for them on those bottles but had no way of examining them. You have?"

"Yes, since Solier employed me as a detective I have tried to live up to the best detective standards."

Falter turned to Maria, who had removed the bowl from the rude stove and was moving toward the door.

"You don't need to do the cooking any more, Maria. Lee will take charge now."

"*Si, señor.*" Her expression did not change.

Falter followed Rennert into the patio.

"I think," he said, "that I'll go to my room and lie down a while. I don't feel very well. The heat has been almost too much for me the last few days. Dinner will be served about six. In the meantime make yourself at home. The living room—the *sala* we call it—is over there to the left of the main entrance. There's a radio."

"Very well, thanks."

Rennert was watching Maria's progress through the flowers toward a door on the north side. He saw her stop once, bend over and remove with careful fingers a withered leaf from the stalk of a red poinsettia.

"One more question while I'm giving vent to my curiosity," he said as he followed Falter into the front patio. "I saw a young Mexican out here this afternoon. I suppose it was Esteban Flores?"

"Yes, he's still waiting for parts for his plane."

Rennert watched Falter's face as he spoke. "He was carrying a black case and a spade when I saw him. It struck me that this was a hot afternoon for digging."

"Oh, that!" Falter smiled. "The young fellow spends his time in the mornings and the late afternoons digging up on the hillside back of the house." He paused at the door of his room and gazed up at the sky. "It seems that that grandfather of his I was telling you about was killed here during the Revolution. They've never found his body. Flores is looking for it."

"This is rather a late date to be doing that, isn't it?"

"Yes, but they dug up the whole place after they came into possession again. No luck. Flores hasn't said much since he's been here but I think he's run across some proof that the body was buried up there on the hill. These old Mexican families are proud as hell, you know, and they think it's a disgrace if some member isn't given Christian burial. Personally, I doubt whether he'll ever find any trace of the old boy."

Rennert walked toward his room, the water bottle held carefully under an arm.

He happened to glance in the window beside his door and stopped stockstill.

Mark Arnhardt was standing upon a chair and reaching over the top of the tall wardrobe. As Rennert watched he drew back his hand and got down. He held an oblong pasteboard box, decorated gaudily with multicolored ribbons.

Rennert opened the door and went in.

7
UNGUESSED DEPTHS

"Hello," Rennert said. A slow flush mounted to Arnhardt's cheeks and he screwed the side of his mouth into a wry smile. He had changed to a white Palm Beach suit that looked too small for his large muscular body. It emphasized, too, the tanned skin of his face and hands.

"Oh, hello, Rennert." He shifted his weight awkwardly from one foot to the other. "I'm intruding again. Sorry. You see," he cleared his throat with unnecessary force, "I wanted to get this box that had been left in here. I knocked but you weren't in so I took the liberty of coming in anyway. Hope you won't mind?" His smile was suddenly pleasant and boyish, breaking the tension of his lips.

"Not at all," Rennert said. "I still feel as if I were imposing on you."

Arnhardt stuffed the box (it looked to Rennert like an ordinary candy box) into a pocket of his coat and stood in the same posture as before, with a thumb hooked about his belt and an arm held out akimbo.

"Won't you sit down?" Rennert invited.

Arnhardt hesitated a moment, let his arm fall and moved toward a chair. He lowered himself into it as if uncertain of its stability. It creaked beneath his weight.

Rennert extended cigarettes.

"No, thanks." Arnhardt brought out a pipe and tobacco pouch. "I'd rather smoke this."

For an interval both were intent upon their lights. Rennert sat opposite Arnhardt and regarded him through a haze of smoke. He saw the brown protruding eyes rest for an instant questioningly upon the water bottle which he had placed on a table.

"I suppose you know, Arnhardt, why I'm here?"

The young man brought his attention quickly back.

"Falter told me that you were here to look after some business for the company."

"Did he tell you anything more explicit?"

"Why, no. But then I never pay much attention to the business side of the company. I let Falter and Solier attend to that. I've been busy lately getting this power plant in shape to supply electricity to the place."

"It has been installed recently?" Rennert asked with some surprise.

"Yes, we just got it in working order last week."

Rennert centered his attention for a moment on his cigarette before he went on: "I was going to explain about that water bottle. I understand that someone has been making away with the drinking water here. Mr. Solier asked me to investigate."

"Oh, that." Arnhardt's eyebrows drew together so that he seemed to be staring at the tip of his pipe. "It *is* peculiar, isn't it? I don't know who could be doing it."

"You don't know of anyone who might be interested in forcing you people to move?"

"No," accompanied by a slow negative movement of the head, "I don't. The whole thing seems senseless. I feel sure, though, that it's someone from outside."

"Why?"

"Well, it stands to reason, doesn't it? Those doors to the patio are never locked. It would be easy enough for someone to come in."

"But the kitchen is locked at night, Falter tells me."

"Yes," Arnhardt thought a moment. "But Maria lost her keys not long ago. Someone might have picked them up."

"Is there anyone living hereabouts?"

"Nobody at all, for miles and miles, that I know of. Of course these hills are full of caves. Someone might be hiding out there and coming in at night for water. Some spring that he had been depending on may have gone dry. That's the only explanation I've been able to think of."

"How long has this been going on?"

"Ever since I've been down here—about two weeks.

"You came down with your stepfather, George Stahl, I understand."

"Yes."

"His death was regrettable. Sunstroke, I believe?"

There was a hint of reserve in Arnhardt's manner and of curtness in his voice as he said: "Yes."

Rennert had the feeling that he was venturing upon exceedingly thin ice that might at any moment precipitate him into unguessed depths. He persisted, however: "You were with him, I believe, after his stroke?"

"Yes." Arnhardt's tone was brittle.

"Falter tells me that he kept talking about the air being yellow."

"Yes. It was the effect of the sun."

"It conveyed no other meaning to you?"

"No. Why should it?" Arnhardt's face was rigid and in the dimming light looked darkly threatening.

Rennert said quietly: "You knew that Miguel was taken sick this afternoon?"

"No."

"He has been confusing the colors of the flowers in his room. They seem yellow to him."

Arnhardt stared straight at Rennert's face for perhaps five seconds. He seemed to choke then and said indistinctly: "Yellow?"

"Yes, the similarity of the two cases struck me as odd."

Arnhardt got slowly to his feet, one hand cramming the pipe into a pocket. His eyes went to the door, as if seeking escape.

"God, this is terrible!" he said in an unsteady voice. "Let me get out in the air and think, will you?"

8
A LIGHTED CANDLE

RENNERT WALKED ALONG a narrow path between scarlet carnations and red and yellow columbines, their colors deepened by the shade.

The rim of the sun was touching the ocherous red tiles of the roof. It had, Rennert thought, an oddly suffused glow, as if he were looking at it through cellophane. The atmosphere seemed heavier, laden with odors of the parched earth and of the many flowers. Not a breath of air stirred the little sea of petals and leaves.

He came to the open door of the Montemayor quarters.

Upon a cot at the opposite side of the room lay an elderly Mexican, his lined face impassive. Rennert thought at first that he was staring at the ceiling but saw in a moment that his eyes were closed. The only movement visible was in his hands, like brown talons, that kept twisting as if in pain at the bedclothes.

On a low table beside him stood a brown pottery bowl filled with red hibiscus flowers.

Deep in an alcove cut in the wall at the head of the bed rested a small wax image of the Virgin of Guadalupe, the hem of her skirt and her feet hidden behind a banked mass of white floripondio blossoms. In front of them a candle burned with a steady flame.

Maria Montemayor was kneeling upon the floor, her gaze fixed upon the wax figure. For at least three minutes, as Rennert stood upon the threshold, there was no movement at all discernible in her body.

He waited—not without a feeling of self-reproach at his intrusion.

She rose finally, her fingers going nimbly through the movements of the cross, and turned. As she saw him her face froze into immobility and a thinly veiled look of hostility sprang into her eyes.

She moved toward him quickly and stood barring the doorway.

"What is it, señor?" Emotion ruffled the flat monotonous surface of her speech.

"Is it permitted to see Miguel?"

She shook her head and threw her shoulders back defensively.

"No, señor, you can do nothing for him."

"You wanted someone to tell him that those flowers were red, not yellow. I thought I would do so."

With one hand she reached backward and closed the door. A vague smile touched her lips without altering the stonelike quality of her face.

"There is no need now, señor. He knows that they are not yellow."

"And the *claveles*? He saw them again?"

"Yes, he saw that they were white."

"He has fear of death no more then?"

"No more, señor."

"He is still suffering?"

She hesitated and the smile died slowly on her lips.

"Yes, señor, he is suffering, but it will pass. It will pass," she repeated with a note of passionate emphasis. "La Guadalupana will aid him. She will drive out—" She stopped and something seemed to close behind her eyes, leaving them as lifeless as obsidian flakes.

"*Los aires?*" Rennert finished for her.

The fingers of one hand plucked at the fringe of the *rebozo*.

"Yes, señor." It was almost inaudible. She half-turned and fumbled for the knob.

"But where did they strike Miguel?" Rennert asked quickly, before the moment of confidence should be gone. "There is little water here."

Her face was averted so that he had to lean forward to catch her words: "I do not know, señor, I do not know."

Before he could continue she was gone and he faced a blank weathered door.

He lit a cigarette and strolled back through the flowers. He knew now that he had interpreted rightly the woman's suppressed fear of that afternoon, her wary glance at the jug of water. *Los aires,* "the airs," are tiny little people, malignant and mischievous, who dwell about water, diving and swimming or merely lying on banks. One must take care to wear amulets of round stones and petrified deer-eyes or they will strike his body, causing illness. One must not mention them by name, either, or they will become angered. The white man accounts for the Empress Carlotta's madness by saying that it was occasioned by grief and anxiety for her husband beleaguered in Querétaro. In Mexico they know better—but say nothing.

He stopped under the archway, staring out over the patio. He was glad that he had no confidant for his thoughts then, for he was fighting off a feeling of un easiness, of vague, undefined foreboding in the face of some dimly sensed danger. In this damned country (he cursed it often yet knew that this feeling of disquiet which it inspired was, perversely, for him an invariable lodestone) one never felt stability. There was always a faint tremor under one's feet, in the air one breathed. As if the volcanoes far to the south were stirring ominously in their sleep.

He was puzzled by the whole affair, by the inexplicable manner in which the mention of yellowness was tingeing with the bizarre the lives of these commonplace people. That there was some link between Stahl's death and Miguel's illness he felt certain. For a moment his mind played with the idea of apparitions, staged by naturalistic means, for the benefit of the susceptible. He could conceive of a man being frightened to death, granted a weak heart and an active imagination. But the physical pain that accompanied this malady—and its prolongation. No, it wouldn't do.

The cigarette was a solace. The weather, he told himself, was doubtless responsible for his feeling. This dead utter stillness that had settled upon everything . . .

He started at a faint insect-like touch upon the back of his neck, turned and saw a tendril, like a blind green worm, swaying toward him in the still air. Behind it, on the vine that coiled over the adobe, an orchid opened a swollen rust-brown mouth.

Good God, he thought, *I'll be gibbering next!*

He stepped into the patio.

A woman—tall, thin, impeccable in black bombazine—stood by the frangipani tree, pulling one of the lower branches toward her. As he watched she detached with deft fingers one of the white flowers, stared at it a moment through gold spectacles, buried her long straight nose in its softness. There was an odd flushed look on her face when she withdrew it that could be (Rennert thought, regarding her through the gathering dimness of evening) nothing but sensuality.

She raised a hand, awkwardly, and fixed the flower in the steel-gray hair over her right ear with the determined movement of a woman thrusting in a hatpin.

Rennert stepped forward.

"Miss Fahn, I believe?"

9
PETALS TIPPED WITH BLOOD

HER FINGERS FUMBLED with the stem of the flower while color mottled her face. Her hand fell to her side, leaving the flower caught in the weblike net that covered her hair. She drew a handkerchief from the side pocket of her dress and daubed at her face.

"Yes?" (Rennert thought of the white-hot dagger-like flare of an acetylene torch.)

"I'm Mr. Rennert, a guest here at the hacienda for a few days. Pardon the brusqueness of my introduction. I was wandering about, admiring the flowers. I saw you and thought I'd get acquainted. I have a package for you—some postcards."

"Oh, yes," the flame flickered out, touching him with a vestige of warmth. "I heard that you were coming down. I'm very glad to know you."

There was an uneasy pause. Composure was sheathing the woman in austere flat planes above which the frangipani blossom, evidently forgotten, nodded grotesquely.

"I'm so glad to get the postcards," she said. "I was afraid that Mr. Solier was *never* going to send them. I don't think he or Mr. Falter realized how important they were."

She seemed to recede for a moment into some private sphere of her own. When she emerged there was a nervous lightness about her manner and her voice was almost chatty: "I was just examining this tree. To my mind it has the most beautiful and the most fragrant flowers of any in Mexico. My profession, you know, allows me such few moments like this."

"I understood you were a botanist," Rennert said. "I've often wondered if you scientists looked at plants and flowers merely as laboratory specimens or if you saw more in them—like we benighted laymen."

"Oh, no, we don't look at them that way, Mr. Rennert. I assure you. We realize the important role they have played in history." (She was shying away determinedly, Rennert knew, from the obvious meaning of his words.) "The diffusion of human culture in all its aspects has always been aided by that of domesticated plants. The civilization of the Mexican plateau, for instance, would not have spread as it did over native America if it hadn't been for the fact that maize was first grown here." She paused as if for breath and looked up at the white blossoms overhead. "And this tree here. Do you know, I almost expect to see blood on its petals every time I look at it. Silly, isn't it?"

Rennert's eyes followed hers. The flowers loomed whitely out of the dark leaves. About them tiny insects buzzed ecstatically. (*She is disturbed*, he thought, *by my presence and is trying to cover it up by this flow of words.*)

"I don't believe I understand, Miss Fahn."

"Oh, of course you don't," she laughed. He saw that her long capable fingers were twisting at a corner of the handkerchief. "It's known here in Mexico as the blood-flower of Montezuma. It's just an old legend."

"I don't believe that I have ever heard it."

"The frangipani tree—that's what this is—comes from the West Indies originally. A specimen of it was brought to Montezuma's brother, who was governor of the province of Yuquane, to the southeast of Mexico City. One of the flowers was taken to Montezuma. Its beauty and fragrance were greater than those of any of the flowers in the royal gardens. So he sent messengers to his brother, demanding the tree. The brother refused. Montezuma, who was used of course to having his own way, offered whole provinces in exchange for it. Still the brother refused. Then Montezuma sent an army into Yuquane, had his brother killed and the tree brought to his gardens. When it was replanted there the tips of the flowers turned red as blood. A symbol, you see, of Montezuma's guilt."

Rennert had been observing her as she talked. He had seen the glow of perspiration on her face and the thin film of moisture that clouded the thick lenses of her spectacles.

"Only in Mexico," he said with what he thought to be appropriate sententiousness, "would one commit fratricide for a flower."

"Yes, flowers do seem to mean so much to the Mexicans, don't they? Maria, the old Mexican woman here, practically lives for her flowers."

"For a botanist, this must be an interesting place."

"It is. I've gotten several ideas from Maria's flowers—about the possibility of adapting varieties found here to the southern part of the United States."

"It must take a great deal of water to keep them in such a flourishing condition."

"Yes, I suppose so."

"Where does she get the water, do you know? I see that the fountain is dry."

"No, I don't know," her voice fell into that dead pause that comes when a person who has been talking with thoughts elsewhere reaches the end of verbal resources.

The low tinkle of chimes echoed through the patio.

An unguarded look of relief came over the woman's face. She glanced at her wristwatch.

"The first call," she said as her fingers folded the handkerchief into a neat square. "Dinner will be served in ten minutes. You'll pardon me? I want to," a barely perceptible pause, "wash my hands."

10
"IN DANGER'S HOUR"

RENNERT OPENED the door of the wardrobe and took a coat from its hanger. Dinner at the hacienda, he had decided, would require it.

As he did so his eyes were on a level with the shelf upon which rested the empty whisky bottle. It had been drained, he saw now, recently, for the sides were moist and a few drops remained in the curvature of the bottom. It was, he supposed, a relic of Arnhardt's occupancy of the room.

As he walked into the patio a radio blared forth, harsh with static, from the door to the left of the entrance. Remembering that it had been designated as the *sala*, he went toward it.

It was a room similar to his own but larger and more pretentious. Large gilt-framed portraits of stiff-whiskered gentlemen adorned the blue-tinted walls. Between the two south windows a wooden image of the Virgin of the Remedies looked down sorrowfully upon two plaster nymphs in lascivious embrace on a round refectory table of polished mosaic inlay. In one of the corners stood a huge-bellied jar of blue-and-white Talavera majolica. There was a fragile-looking gilt-and-satin sofa and stiff straight chairs with graceful pipestem legs.

An intruder in the midst of this antiquated elegance, a radio set stood against the west wall: a transmitter in a tall cabinet of baked wrinkled enamel and a receiver beside it on a low bench.

Mark Arnhardt sat wide-legged on a stool before the receiver. He was hunched forward, twirling the dial, so that his broad shoulders strained at the seams of his coat. Thin strains of music filtered through the crackle of static.

He looked around, saw Rennert, and got to his feet.

"Hello, Mr. Rennert, come in and sit down." The intent to inject hospitable heartiness into his voice was obvious.

He glanced toward the other side of the room, where the young Mexican whom Rennert had seen that afternoon sat by the window, idly turning over the pages of an illustrated magazine.

"Mr. Rennert, this is Mr. Flores."

The Mexican rose with alacrity, dropped the magazine and came forward with extended hand and a set smile on his dark olive face. He wore now a dark blue suit with a pinstripe of green, a light green shirt, and a maroon and orange tie.

"Delighted, Mr. Rennert, I am sure." His English was almost perfect, made noticeable only by a certain softness of intonation and a faint lingering on the vowels.

His hand was soft and faintly moist, with a heavy signet ring, and Rennert's sensitive nose caught the scent of pomade and perfume.

"Will you not sit down?" Flores indicated a chair on the other side of the enraptured nymphs.

Rennert sat down.

Arnhardt stood for a moment, awkwardly, as if trying to think of something to say. He dropped onto the stool again and remarked over his shoulder: "The static's fierce tonight. We must be in for a change of weather."

With a cambric handkerchief the Mexican delicately removed perspiration from his forehead.

"It is the humidity," he said, "that comes before a storm in this part of Mexico." As if he had fulfilled a conversational duty by his acquiescence with Arnhardt's statement he turned his head and regarded Rennert with open interest. "Mr. Falter told me that you were going to be with us for a time. You are from San Antonio, I believe?"

"Yes."

"Ah, a beautiful city, San Antonio. I have spent much time there, on my way to and from the university."

"You've been attending school in the United States?"

"Yes, at the Kansas Agricultural and Mechanical College." He paused at the end of each sentence as if mentally jotting down a period before proceeding. "I am studying engineering. That is my plane out on the grounds. I was forced down while on my way back to Mexico City. I have had to wait for extra parts to be sent. Several of them I was unable to get in Mexico City and am waiting for them to be shipped from the United States."

"Unfortunate," Rennert said.

Flores smiled pleasantly, revealing white pearl-like teeth.

"Not at all. I have enjoyed my stay here on the hacienda. Mr. Falter and Mr. Arnhardt have been most hospitable." He paused and seemed to be arranging into words the next thought that he wanted to express. "You know, Mr. Rennert, that my most early childhood recollections are of this place. I was born here and lived here until the Revolution. We went then, my family and I, to the United States until it was over. You have looked over the hacienda?"

"Not closely, no."

"If you will look at the walls on both sides of the door you will see the holes of bullets. They are from the time when the bandits captured the hacienda. My grandfather died then. He could have gone with us to safety but he did not wish to desert the family property."

He spoke in an unimpassioned voice but Rennert observed the gleam of pride in the dark deepset eyes and the lifting of the chin below the too-masculine mustache.

"Good evening, everyone," the words were an obbligato to a determined ripple of chimes.

Miss Fahn came into the room. She walked on feet clad in low-heeled shoes that squeaked audibly and laced tightness held her body in uncompromising rigidity yet she managed to put into her entrance some of the effect that Rennert had always associated with the expression "sweeping into a room." It was more, he decided, than the nicety with which she stopped, equidistant from the three of them, and the manner of an alert hostess with which she looked about her.

"Have any of you," she asked, "seen Mr. Falter?"

"Not for an hour or so." Rennert got to his feet.

She looked down at her watch as if it were the arbiter in a momentous question which concerned them all.

"It is time for dinner," she said.

"Is Mr. Falter not in his room?" Flores asked as he stood with an air of patient boredom.

"He doesn't seem to be. I knocked but he didn't answer."

Arnhardt remained seated at the radio, the broad expanse of his back deliberately (Rennert felt) indifferent to the query.

Static grated deafeningly into a string quartet's rendition of "Cielito Lindo."

Arnhardt turned the dial again. There was abrupt cessation of noise and an announcer's voice, weirdly clear, knife-sharp in the hot still air:

"You are listening to station WARE, *the voice of the Border, on the Rio Grande."*

A long pause filled with a low humming as of a tautened wire in the wind.

"We have just received word that the tropical hurricane which has been lashing the Gulf of Mexico has unexpectedly turned inland in the direction of Tampico. Storm warnings have been posted along the coast from Brownsville to Vera Cruz. During the next half hour station WARE *will sign off, to clear the air for possible distress signals from coastwise shipping caught in the path of the hurricane."*

Their eyes remained riveted on the lighted dial for a moment after the clear urgent voice had ceased. Despite their familiarity with the radio that voice, seeking them out in a hidden pocket of the mountains, had seemed so close that—aside from the disturbing implications of the message—it left a momentary hush upon the room.

"How terrible!" Miss Fahn spoke into the silence. "Those poor people down in Tampico. How helpless they must feet, knowing that storm is coming toward them. And the people on ships—"

There was a tightness about her lips that robbed her voice of its note of artificiality. "Shall we go in to dinner," she said.

As they walked into the patio Rennert found himself walking by her side as Arnhardt and Flores brought up the rear.

She said as they made their way along the paving-stones: "It must be that storm which is causing the humidity in the air to-night."

"Yes. Tampico is less than two hundred miles away, you know."

She looked at him quickly.

"You don't suppose there's any danger of the storm reaching here?"

"Oh, no, I don't think so." Rennert put reassurance into his voice. "If it does its force will have been broken by the mountains." (He thought: *I'm not sure at all It would require more of a barrier than the range which lies between us and the coast to assure us of safety from the vagaries of a tropical hurricane*.)

"A storm," Miss Fahn said, "always alarms me so. My brother died in one. His ship went down somewhere in the China Sea. I believe they call them typhoons there. I have never wanted to look at the ocean again."

They had come to the door of Falter's apartment. She turned her head (Rennert felt that she was glad of the excuse to do so) and waited until Arnhardt and Flores came up.

"You might go in and knock on his bedroom door, Mr. Arnhardt. He may have been asleep and not have heard me."

Arnhardt shrugged.

"If he can't keep track of the time let him miss out on a meal," he said gruffly and stalked on.

"I will go if you wish," Flores said.

He went in while Rennert and Miss Fahn waited. After a moment she walked to the edge of the paving and, with an attempt at casualness which did not deceive him, looked up at the sky.

The Tolmans were walking slowly along the west side of the patio, the girl's hand resting lightly in the crook of her husband's elbow. Neither was talking.

Flores came out and said without his usual smile: "Mr. Falter will be with us in a moment. He is not feeling well."

"Oh." Miss Fahn's teeth sank very gently into her lower lip. "Let us walk on," she said to Rennert.

They met the Tolmans by the dining-room door.

"Good evening, Mrs. Tolman. Good evening, Mr. Tolman," there was agitation beneath the formality of Miss Fahn's voice. "Have you folks met Mr. Rennert?"

"Yes," Tolman answered, "we've had the pleasure." He had on a well-worn linen suit. In a glance Rennert's practiced eye took in the careful pressing to which it had been subjected and the little spot on the cuff where the coat had been neatly mended. The man's face bore a pleasant, rather abstracted smile but on each cheekbone was visible a hectic flush.

Ann Tolman's eyes met Rennert's for an instant as she murmured: "Good evening, Mr. Rennert." She wore a printed frock whose crispness and freshness did not quite make up for the white drained look on her face. Rennert noted the quickness with which her gaze left him to travel to Arnhardt, who was standing to one side, his back and one foot propped against the wall, and staring straight ahead of him.

"Hasn't it been warm today?" Miss Fahn was saying in a preoccupied manner, half her attention on Falter's door. "I thought it would be, so I told Maria this morning to prepare a salad for dinner tonight, something crisp. Her ideas of salads are really impossible."

Ann brought her attention back: "But didn't you know that Lee had returned?"

"Lee?" Miss Fahn frowned. "No, I didn't. I'd hoped that we had gotten rid of him for good. Maria's cooking may be lacking in some respects but I always feel—well, so much more comfortable if she's in the kitchen. I feel so much freer to give her suggestions. Well, here comes Mr. Falter at last."

Something about the sharp way she said it made Rennert turn. He saw at once that something was wrong.

"Shall we go in?" Miss Fahn said hurriedly to Rennert. As he escorted her into the room she whispered: "It's perfectly obvious what the trouble is. This has happened before but never so bad as this. It will be better if we pretend that we don't notice it." She raised her voice and indicated the chair on her right. "You may take this place, Mr. Rennert."

As Rennert held her chair for her he was observing Falter, who was making his way to the opposite end of the long table. The man's face was gray ash beneath his tan and little beads of perspiration glistened on his forehead. He stood for a moment, one hand gripping the edge of the table, and stared straight at a bowl of white carnations in the center. He dropped heavily into his chair.

Rennert took his place beside Arnhardt. Flores sat beyond the latter and, on the opposite side, the Tolmans. Rennert was feeling decidedly uneasy. Falter wasn't drunk, he knew that. He was in pain, however, and, unless he read his face wrongly, was keeping himself going by sheer force of will.

The kitchen door creaked and Lee came into the room with a soup-laden tray.

Miss Fahn glanced at him and frowned.

"Lee!" her voice was imperative. "Haven't you forgotten something?"

Lee looked at her. His face was blank but his eyes glittered as they reflected the light of the unshaded electric bulb.

"No, miss, not forget anything. Soup all hot. Burn like—"

She checked him with an uplifted hand.

"That will do, Lee. I am referring to your white jacket. Didn't I tell you always to wear it when you were serving? Please go and put it on at once."

The steaming bowls tilted perilously as the Chinaman began to shift his hands.

"Too hot, miss, to wear goddamned jacket. Kitchen hot like—"

"That's enough, Lee. Please go and put that jacket on. Do it before you serve the soup."

Lee's lips moved soundlessly, the soup slid toward the other end of the tray and he turned back into the kitchen.

"So trying," Miss Fahn was saying to Rennert in an undertone, "to preserve the conventions in a country like this." She went on, something about "keeping servants in their places" and "Englishmen who always dress for dinner, even in the tropics." Rennert was thinking: *She is a little girl in pigtails, playing at keeping house and aping with the air of a grande dame a world that isn't hers.* Then she was clearing her throat and addressing the table: "Did you hear the dreadful news that just came over the radio? About the hurricane that was due to strike Tampico this evening? I think that a prayer would be appropriate—a prayer for the safety of those who are upon the sea tonight, whose lives are in danger."

She lowered her chin to rest upon a cameo brooch and in the strained hush that fell upon them began to intone: "Eternal Father, strong to save, whose arm doth bind the restless wave . . ."

Rennert ventured a glance about the table.

Arnhardt was leaning back in his chair, staring across the carnations in the Talavera jar at Ann Tolman's hair, to which the electric light was lending a metallic sheen. (Rennert's eyes narrowed thoughtfully. There was something almost fierce about the intensity of the young man's gaze and a softness, in that unguarded moment, about the rough outlines of his face.)

". . . the mighty ocean deep its own appointed limits keep . . ."

Flores sat upright in his chair, as with one hand he marshalled knife and fork and spoon into position. There was an openly derisive smile on his lips.

Stephen Tolman held his head slightly inclined but was regarding Falter sideways.

". . . hear us when we cry to Thee, for those in peril on the sea . . ."

The fingers of both Falter's hands were grasping the tablecloth, their tendons white against the tight skin. The cords of his temples stood out, glistening with perspiration.

". . . who didst brood upon the chaos dark and rude . . ."

A chair crashed against the tiles.

Miss Fahn raised her head, a startled look on her face.

Falter had gotten to his feet and was swaying to and fro. He raised a hand and brushed it across his eyes.

"What's the matter with these lights?" he demanded thickly.

"Why, nothing at all, Mr. Falter." Miss Fahn's voice was edged with acerbity. "If you will just sit down—"

He took away his hand and fixed, with difficulty, his eyes on the electric light.

"Who in the hell," he said, "put a yellow bulb in there?"

He fell forward. An outstretched hand struck the Talavera jar, overturning it and the white carnations.

11
SICK ROOM

ANN TOLMAN CLOSED the door of Falter's bedroom noiselessly behind her and faced Rennert. She raised both her hands and buried her fingers in her hair, pushing it slowly upward. The movement stretched the skin tight over her cheekbones and gave her eyes a wild terror-filled look.

"He's suffering," she said, "terribly. I don't know any way to relieve him. You still want to talk to him?"

"Yes, if you don't think it would harm him." Rennert was watching her closely. After he and Arnhardt had half-carried, half-guided Falter to his room she had quietly and competently assumed the role of nurse, issuing orders for quiet and gently assisting in his undressing. If, Rennert thought, she were to crack up now there was no one to whom he could turn for clear-headed assistance.

"I told him," she spoke in a strained voice. "He wants to see you. I'll wait out here."

Rennert went inside.

Falter lay with one hand thrown over his eyes. Ann had cupped a piece of paper over the electric bulb so that its light was directed against the ceiling, leaving the bed in shadow.

Rennert sat upon the edge of a chair.

"Mr. Falter?" He spoke softly.

Falter took away his hand and looked at him for a moment dazedly.

"Hello, Rennert." He spoke hoarsely. "Glad you're here. This is pretty bad."

"You are in pain?"

"Yes. Stomach mostly. And Rennert—"

"Yes?"

"That light bulb wasn't yellow, was it?"

"No, it wasn't."

A pause while a hand pulled clumsily at the front of his perspiration-dampened pajamas.

"Then I know how Stahl felt."

"Want to tell me about it?"

"I got sick a little before dinner. Came in and lay down. All of a sudden everything was yellow. Like a weak yellow light had been turned on. It got worse. When I went in to the dining room I could hardly see." He raised himself on an elbow and stared at Rennert, the muscles of his face working. "Rennert, you know what this means?"

"Yes?"

"Poison, man, poison!" His voice rose. "First Stahl, then Miguel, then myself. If I'd only had sense enough to see it before! I'd have shot the bastard, whoever he is."

"And who," Rennert asked, "do you think is doing it?"

Falter lay back on the pillow, his eyes fixed on the ceiling.

"I don't know," his voice was choked. "I'm not sure, that is."

"The possibilities are rather limited, you know."

"Yes. Only two."

"Two?"

"Arnhardt and Tolman. Arnhardt and I have never gotten along. He thought he could step in and have as much say-so about running this place as I. He's in love with that Tolman girl, too. She has worked on his sympathies. Told him that we framed her husband—Solier and I—on that San Antonio deal."

"I don't believe I know about that."

"Tolman was working for us then, collecting rents and notes. There was a shortage in the funds. We didn't press any charges of embezzlement. Knew the fellow was hard up. Brought him down here so that he could draw our plans for us."

"Has Tolman ever made any threats?"

"No, but I suppose he might be too smart for that."

"But what advantage would it be to him to make attempts on yours and Stahl's lives?"

"His way of getting even."

Rennert thought a moment.

"But Miguel?" he asked. "Why should Tolman or Arnhardt or anyone else want to poison him?" Falter was silent for a long time.

"I don't know," he said at last. "There's no reason that I know of."

"You have been bothered with stomach trouble for some time, I believe?"

"Yes, ever since I came down to this damned country."

"Has it been getting any worse lately?"

"Since I ran out of those tablets, yes."

"Tell me what you ate or drank this afternoon."

"Nothing except that whisky."

"While I was with you?"

"Yes."

"But I drank out of the same bottle."

"Yes." It seemed to come reluctantly from Falter's thick throat. "That's so."

"You didn't drink any more after I left?"

"No."

"And those tablets—you took no more of them?"

"Yes, one more. After I left you in the patio."

"You and I were gone for perhaps fifteen minutes, when we went to the kitchen with Lee. Where was the box of tablets during that time?"

"On the desk out in the office."

"It was in the same place when you came back as when you left?"

"I think so. I didn't notice particularly. I took one more and put the box in the upper drawer of the desk."

"Was the taste of the second one you took like that of the first?"

"I didn't notice any difference. They're bitter as hell. You think that someone may have come in while we were gone and poisoned them?"

"It looks as if that were the only answer." Rennert got to his feet. "I'm going to talk to Solier now on the radio. I'll have him send a doctor down. Is there anything I can do for you?"

With an effort Falter moved so that he lay on his side.

"I'd like some water—cool water."

"I'll have Mrs. Tolman bring it to you. Let me know if there's anything else."

"All right, Rennert. Thanks."

Ann Tolman was standing by the window of the outer room, staring out into the patio. She turned as Rennert came out.

"Mr. Falter would like some water. Would you mind getting it for him?"

"Of course not. You'll stay here in case he wants anything? It will only take a moment."

"Yes."

When she had gone Rennert went to the desk and opened the top drawer. The box of tablets which he had given to Falter that afternoon lay in one corner. He took it out and held it to the light. Upon the top of it was pasted the label of a San Antonio drug store bearing the typewritten name of a physician and a number. He took out an envelope, shook several of the white tablets into it and returned it, carefully folded, to his pocket. As he put the box back into place his eyes rested on the holster of tooled leather that filled most of the space. From it protruded the butt of a pistol. It was, he saw as he half-drew it out, a Colt automatic.

He was closing the drawer when Ann Tolman came back into the room carrying a jug of water and a glass.

"There's a question I'd like to ask you, Mrs. Tolman."

"Yes?"

"It's about George Stahl's death. Do you remember whether or not he kept talking about things being yellow up to the time of his death?"

"Oh, no," she answered readily. "That was only at first, after they had brought him in out of the sun. He seemed to get his normal eyesight back after an hour or so."

"Thank you," Rennert said. "I'll go now. Call me in case you need me."

"Mr. Rennert," she checked his movement of departure with a low controlled voice, "I want to thank you for having kept still about this afternoon. I feel that I owe you an explanation. When we have time to talk I'll tell you—I'll try to tell you, that is—about it."

Before he could reply she had gone.

12
STATIC

"STATION XADY, MEXICO, calling station W10XAKI, San Antonio. Station XADY, Mexico, calling station W10XAKI, San Antonio. Station XADY. . ."

Rennert stood before the transmitter and kept up the call at regularly spaced intervals.

His eyes went to the window, within whose narrow frame the stark ramparts to the south were crimson with sun and rocks and stunted trees and phallic cathedral-cactus were hazed softly in mauve.

The desolate grandeur of the sight and his position at the instrument emphasized his remoteness and the tenuous link that connected him with the world beyond the mountains. Suppose one of these wires or tubes were to refuse service. There would remain nothing but wasteland between him and the nearest town that hugged the ribbon of lonely highway.

". . . calling station W10XAKI, San Antonio."

The answer came suddenly, eerily out of the brittle crackle of atmospherics: "Station W10XAKI, San Antonio, answering station XADY, Mexico."

"Solier?"

"Yes, Mr. Rennert. Glad to know you got there safely. How was the trip?"

"Not too bad. I'm afraid that I must report a serious state of affairs here at the hacienda."

"What's the matter?" It was the first time the hollow disembodied voice had altered its mechanical tone.

"Both Mr. Falter and Miguel Montemayor were taken ill this afternoon. I believe their condition is serious."

"Montemayor?" A pause. "What does the trouble seem to be?"

"It seems to be poisoning although I can't as yet determine the nature. In my opinion they need medical attention immediately, before the night is over if possible. I wondered if it would be possible to send a doctor down here?"

"I don't know. The place is so isolated—"

"You can at least get a message down to Monterrey or Victoria."

"I'll try."

"I want to impress upon you, Mr. Solier, the need for haste."

"Exactly what happened?"

"Montemayor was ill when I arrived. Falter's attack came at the dinner-table, about forty-five minutes ago. A curious circumstance, that you might mention to the doctor, is that both of them have had the illusion at first that objects about them were yellow. The doctor may know of some illness or poisoning of which this is a symptom."

"What was that? Yellow?"

"Yes."

There was a long pause.

Solier's voice came again as if from a phonograph record over whose grooves a worn needle was grating: "I'll tell the doctor, Mr. Rennert. You mean that they are out of their minds?"

"No, I don't think so. I believe that something actually happened to their sight. The same thing, I am told, occurred when George Stahl was brought in out of the sun."

"George Stahl? You're sure of that?"

"Falter and Arnhardt and Mrs. Tolman all recall it. I don't think it can be a coincidence."

"It doesn't seem likely. Everything else all right down there?"

"I haven't had time to do more than get the lay of the land as yet. I have the feeling, though, that things have about reached the breaking point here."

"What do you mean?"

Rennert found it difficult to explain to this black metal ear just what he did mean. He said: "There's a tension here, an undercurrent of repressed emotions that rather worries me. It's like sitting on top of a volcano."

"That's not very definite, Mr. Rennert. I hope you aren't letting your nerves run away with you."

"I'm not. I know it sounds vague but it's hard to put my feeling into words."

"What about the water?"

"Another bottle disappeared last night."

"Any ideas about that yet?"

Rennert hesitated.

"I think I have a very definite lead but I want to investigate a little more before I commit myself."

"All right, do as you think best. I'll stand by the radio until nine o'clock in case anything develops. And I'll try to get hold of a doctor as soon as possible."

"Thank you, Mr. Solier. Good-by."

"Say—Rennert—"

"Yes?"

"You have a gun?"

"Yes."

Static splintered the words: "Don't hesitate to use it if anything happens. I'll straighten matters up with the Mexican authorities."

"I shan't hesitate, Mr. Solier."

"Well, then—good-by."

"Good-by."

13
DEATH'S INSTRUMENTS

RENNERT SAT for a long time, staring at the silenced radio. He was trying to sort into orderly arrangement the strands that lay tangled at his fingertips. His mind, however, kept grasping stubbornly at some illusive memory that dangled just out of its reach.

It had been the mention of a doctor that had brought it so tantalizingly near. A tiresome discursive little American doctor with whom he had traveled one day, years before, out of the hot brooding land about Vera Cruz, where the sun and the air and the hostile tropical soil take toll of human life. The doctor, relieving his loneliness with talk while Rennert sat in drowsy inattention, had mentioned (he was positive of it) the word "yellow." . . .

He turned around at a light footfall on the tiles.

Esteban Flores was crossing the room.

"I beg your pardon, Mr. Rennert. I came to get the magazine that I was reading before dinner."

He picked it up and began to crease the paper with long dexterous fingers.

"Mr. Falter," he asked softly, "how is he?"

"I haven't any medical knowledge but he seems to be in a very serious condition."

The Mexican lowered himself onto the arm of a chair, carefully adjusting the knife-edge crease of his trouser legs.

"They tell me that old Miguel Montemayor is sick, too."

"Yes, also seriously."

The young man's face was polished granite in the weak glow of the light.

"Do you know what the trouble is?"

"No, I'm sorry to say."

"Mr. Falter's words about the yellow light bulb—what did he mean?"

"I wondered myself. Did it suggest anything to you?"

Flores shook his head slowly.

"Nothing. I thought at first that he was joking—How do you say?—kidding Miss Fahn because she was praying so long. Now, I do not know."

"You know this hacienda and its history. Have you ever heard of any sickness about here that had any connection with the color yellow?" (*That memory, that association with the doctor's conversation—what was it?*)

"No. Down along the coast, about Tampico, there is much yellow fever."

"No, that won't do. Whatever this is, it gives its victims the strange illusion that objects they see are yellow."

The young man's face was grim and his laugh sounded hollow.

"Mr. Rennert, we of this hacienda have known little of sickness. The bullet and the machete have been our surgeons. They operate only once. Their patients are never troubled again—with anything."

"Your family has lived here for a long time, has it not?"

Flores stirred on the chair-arm and laid one leg over the other. His hands held the magazine motionless and the signet ring caught and reflected the light. He fixed Rennert with the steady scrutiny of his eyes.

"One of my ancestors came here with Francisco de Urdiñola in the sixteenth century. We have been here ever since. This house was built by my grandfather, Toledano Flores." Something stirred in his eyes—something (Rennert would have sworn) calculating, as if he were measuring an adversary. "You have heard of my grandfather?"

"Yes, a brave man, I understand."

"A very brave man, Mr. Rennert." There was a pause and he said, his lips forming the words very carefully: "I am looking for his body, Mr. Rennert."

"Strange that it was never found."

"Yes. Shall I tell you the story, Mr. Rennert?"

"If you wish. I thought the subject might be unpleasant for you."

"Unpleasant? No, it does not pain us to speak of him. We are proud that he died rather than leave his property to bandits. I shall tell you." There was a persistence about his manner that rather puzzled Rennert. "They stole—the bandits—all that they could lay their hands on. Miguel and Maria they locked in a hut that used to stand on the hill, where the powerhouse is now. They threatened to set fire to it, if they interfered. They tortured my grandfather to make him tell where the family plate and jewels were hidden. My father and mother had taken them to the United States but they would not believe this. They thought they were hidden somewhere in the mountains. They staked him to the walls, with bayonets through his shoulders, and tortured him. The little Montemayor watched and told afterwards how the old man laughed at them and cursed them."

"The little Montemayor—Miguel and Maria's son?"

"Yes, I forgot that you did not know. He died this spring with a trouble of the intestines—helminthiasis. The little fellow ran away and hid in the hills until the bandits had gone. When he came back and let his father and mother out there was no trace of my grandfather. Miguel thought that he had been killed and buried somewhere near but could find no trace of the body. Maria was very ill afterwards. She had known of the torture, you see."

"Her mind was affected, they say."

Flores shrugged.

"So they say, Mr. Rennert. She became very gentle and sad, like a little child. Since her own son died she spends all her time with her flowers. I think," he hesitated, "that she feels that he is living again in them."

"Living again?"

"Yes. You see, Mr. Rennert, they buried her son under the flowers in the inner patio. But I was telling you of my grandfather. After the Revolution my father came back and searched for the body but could find nothing. There was a story among the peons that the old man had lost his mind during the torture and had run away into the mountains. Some of them even said that they had seen him at the mouth of a cave. My father went and looked. Someone had been living there recently, yes, but there was no trace of my grandfather."

"You think there is still hope in looking?"

"My father has heard a story—from a man in Mexico City—about another man who died there not long ago. This man had been a peon of my grandfather's but joined the bandits. He said that they had killed my grandfather but had not bothered to bury him. This man stayed after they left and buried him on the hillside behind this house. He put a large rock over the grave so that the coyotes would not dig into it. He was ashamed, you see, of what had been done.

"Of course," Flores' eyes were fixed with a peculiar intentness on Rennert's face, "it may be nothing but a story. One hears so many of them in Mexico. But since I am here on the hacienda I am searching. It may take a long time but," he shrugged, "this company—Falter, Solier, and Stahl—got this land so cheap that they can afford to entertain me a few weeks without charge."

Rennert thought: *Mexicans are poor actors. He had some purpose in telling me of his grandfather and of the torture. I wonder what it was.* He said: "I understood the company paid your father a good price for the property."

"A mere ten thousand pesos, Mr. Rennert. Do you call that a good price? Less than three thousand dollars."

"Not exactly."

"That is what they paid. My father took it because he was in need of money at the time and because under this government it is impossible for an *hacendado* to live."

Rennert had gotten up and strolled to the door, where he stood gazing out over the flowers. The shade that had fallen upon them seemed to have metamorphosed them strangely. The shade, deepening their hues, or an odd chiaroscuro effect of the light that shimmered over the upper surfaces of their petals. A hummingbird poised over a scarlet "rain of fire" with a whirr of wings like breath on paper. Tiny twilight insects darted about in swift sibilant confusion, creating by their invisibility the illusion that the flowers themselves were stirring and gasping in the humid still air.

A sea-green worm crept from between two of the paving-stones and moved with awkward contortions of its swollen body toward the shelter of the yellow marigolds and their green leaves.

. . . a worm . . . the yellow of the marigolds . . . green . . .

Memory stirred at last. . . .

Behind him the static tore at the entrails of the radio, disrupting thought, and out of the torture of metal an announcer's voice was saying, just coherent:

"Communication with Tampico has not yet been established so that we are unable to give our listeners any account of the damage done there by the tropical hurricane which struck the city late this afternoon. The hurricane is reported to have continued its way inland in a general southwest-northeast direction at a velocity . . ."

Static drowned the rest.

14
WHITE POISON

MARK ARNHARDT WAS LEANING against the bowl of the fountain, his pipe glowing like a steadily fanned coal and lending his face in the vague half-light a sombre brooding expression.

"Hullo, Rennert," he said without taking the pipe from his mouth. "This weather's fierce, isn't it?"

"Something does seem to be wrong with the cool desert nights one reads about."

"Usually it begins to get cooler as soon as the sun goes down. Tonight it seems to be getting hotter. Wonder if you've got the same feeling I have?"

"How's that?"

"As if—well, as if you were corked up in a bottle, with hot heavy air pressing against the sides, trying to smash in."

"That describes my feeling perfectly," Rennert said. (*It was more than that. The glass was slowly softening into the plasticity that precedes melting and he was staring through its blurred translucence at the edges of the roof sloping up into the ominously darkening sky.*)

"Must be the effects of that storm down on the Gulf. How's Falter?" veering abruptly.

"Very ill."

Arnhardt smoked for a moment in silence, his eyes taking on some of the concentrated fervor of the smoldering tobacco. Rennert could sense a slow tautening of muscles in his solidly planted body.

"Rennert," he said through teeth tight upon the amber, "I'm worried."

"Yes?" Rennert waited.

Arnhardt jerked the pipe from his mouth, showering his trousers with embers. He slapped them off with one hand. His voice came as if muffled by the stagnant air: "Something's wrong here! Wrong as hell!"

"I agree with you. Do you want to talk to me about it now?"

A long silence ended with the sharp tapping of the pipestem against the stone.

"Is there any special reason why I should?" It was singularly devoid of hostility or of any feeling whatever.

"That's for you to decide."

Arnhardt drew a pouch from his hip pocket and deliberately filled his pipe. He seemed to take an unnecessarily long time in cramming the tobacco down.

"Are you a private detective, Rennert?" he asked, apparently absorbed in the movements of his fingers.

"No," Rennert laughed shortly, "although I'm acting in that capacity now. I am an agent of the Customs Bureau of the United States Treasury Department. On furlough, as it were."

"Acting for Solier?"

"My position is not very well defined but it is my understanding that I am acting for the company of which Solier forms a part. That includes, of course, you and Falter as well."

"I see. Then I can talk to you frankly and in confidence?"

"Certainly."

"All right," Arnhardt looked at him over the flare of a match, "I'll talk." He flipped the match into the flowers and stood up. "Let's go outside where there's no danger of being overheard."

"Very well." Rennert said with deliberate intent: "I have in my room some whisky that I brought from Monterrey, in case you'd like a drink."

"No, thanks. I never touch it." Arnhardt laughed. "I suppose you think it strange to find an American in Mexico who doesn't drink?"

"Not at all. My ideas about Americans in Mexico aren't based entirely on observation of the American colony in Mexico City."

"I've heard they're a bunch of sots. Well, it makes no difference to me one way or the other. I just don't, that's all."

They walked side by side through the doorway into the open grounds, flooded by the last of the day's sunlight.

"The reason I suggested a drink," Rennert said, "was because I saw a whisky bottle in the wardrobe of your room—the room, that is, that I dispossessed you of."

"A whisky bottle? Oh, yes, that's been there a long time. It was there when I moved in. I never touched it, though."

"It's empty now." Rennert slowed his steps.

"Well? I'm not a detective but I should say that somebody drank it then." It was an ineffectual attempt at humor, seemingly.

Arnhardt led the way to a stone bench under a tall yucca tree a few feet from the southeast corner of the house.

Over the tiled roof behind them the sky was clear, shot with purple ultramarine, but ahead of them clouds were banked low on the horizon, indistinguishable from the ranges that extended gulfward.

"Clouding up, isn't it?"

The palette of the sky was lost for the moment on Rennert. He asked: "When was the last time you were in that room before I arrived?"

"Early this afternoon, soon after lunch. I went into the *sala* to listen to the radio. There was so much static I turned it off. I went to sleep, must have slept an hour or so. When I woke up I went out to the powerhouse. I must have been there when you came."

"Could you tell me when was the last time you saw that bottle with whisky in it?"

Arnhardt clasped a knee between his hands and frowned in thought.

"I wouldn't swear to it, because I've gotten so used to seeing the bottle there, but I'm fairly sure there was whisky in it when I left. I kept a box of matches up on that shelf. Before I went out I got a handful. I think I would have noticed it if the bottle hadn't been just as it always was—about a fourth full."

He held the pipe tightly gripped but was not drawing on it.

"I see what you mean," he said in a constrained far-away voice. "Someone drank that whisky after I left. Falter or Miguel. They're both sick now."

"Falter had whisky of his own in his room."

"Miguel, then. He moved my things out." Arnhardt bent forward in a hunched attitude and stared straight ahead of him. "Poison!" it had an ugly sound, the way he said it, as if he were putting into the syllables the essence of his antipathy.

"Yes," Rennert said, "I have no doubt that is what it was."

"So," Arnhardt said slowly, "I'm the logical suspect. I poisoned the whisky, knowing that Miguel would probably take a drink of it when he saw it there. I also poisoned Falter. Probably the same way. That's what you're thinking, isn't it?"

"I don't jump at conclusions that quickly."

"I wouldn't blame you if you did. All I can say is that I didn't do it. You can believe me or not."

"Don't you think you might be a little franker with me than you were this afternoon, Arnhardt? Remember that your stepfather's death is linked up apparently with the illness of these two men."

"Because of the symptoms—the recurrence of the yellow vision?"

"Yes."

"That, of course, might be a coincidence."

"It might, yes."

"But you don't think it is."

"No. Do you?"

"I wish to God I could!" It was suddenly a young voice stripped of defensive hardness and, perhaps without being aware of it, seeking companionship. "I've got to have someone to talk to, Rennert. Some one I can trust. I'm going to trust you."

Rennert said nothing. There was no necessity and the utter hush that lay on the desert and the mountains and the leaves above them made words momentous things.

"This is the first time I've admitted to anyone that my stepfather, George Stahl, was murdered." Arnhardt's voice quickened. "At first I took it for granted that it was sunstroke. There wasn't any reason to think otherwise. His talk about things being yellow—well, I didn't think anything about that. I supposed it was the sunlight he was talking about. I took his body back to Amarillo, Texas, as you know. It wasn't until I was on the train coming back that I had time to think. I still remember it as vividly as if it had happened last night." He held his chin propped upon his hand so that the words came slightly distorted. "It was one night while I was lying in my berth wide awake. It came over me all of a sudden that I wasn't satisfied with the sunstroke explanation. It was too simple. And a man who is suffering from sunstroke doesn't have the symptoms that Stahl showed."

"What were they?" Rennert asked quietly.

"Pains—terrible convulsive pains—in the stomach and intestines. Vomiting. Fever. And—that illusion about things being yellow."

"That passed, didn't it?"

"Yes, after a while. Why?"

"It did in Miguel's case. But go ahead."

"Well, I began to think then about the circumstances. I remembered that Stahl had eaten lunch with the rest of us and hadn't touched anything we hadn't. Except afterwards. I'd gone to his room with him and he'd eaten some candy. Caramels. He had always liked them, especially this kind made by Wong's in Mexico City, and had brought a box of them from Monterrey. He offered me some but I was smoking and didn't take any. I left him then. About an hour later I found him in the patio. He died that night."

"There was no post-mortem?"

"No. A doctor came up from Victoria and certified to sunstroke so there was no difficulty about getting the body across the border. But I was telling you about those caramels. When I packed up his things to take back to Amarillo I slipped the box into a compartment of my own grip. I don't know just why. I only stayed until the funeral was over then came right back down here. I hadn't even unpacked so the caramels were still there. The next morning I got them out and examined them. It was a new box. Only two were gone, the ones that Stahl had eaten. The next one in the same row looked as if it had been handled. I started to cut it open. It fell apart and I could see that it had been cut open before and pressed together again. In the center was a white powder."

"What was its appearance?"

"Small crystalline grains. I'll show it to you."

"You still have it then?"

"Yes, it's in the box with the others. That's what I was getting from the top of the wardrobe in your room when you came in this afternoon."

"You never had the candy examined?"

"No." Arnhardt hesitated. "I hid it until I could make up my mind what to do. I didn't decide until tonight."

Rennert tried to keep reprimand out of his words.

"But you could have shown the powder to a chemist or a druggist. You would not necessarily have implicated anyone."

Arnhardt's voice sounded all at once sick: "But I haven't told you everything yet. There were fingerprints on that caramel."

15
A BOX OF CARAMELS

FAR TO THE SOUTHEAST lightning was a thin dagger of fire touching the mountain tops and splashing their crests with sullen crimson.

Arnhardt seemed to be staring at the lightning as he said: "Fingerprints are definite evidence, you know."

"Incontrovertible," Rennert said. "But they might possibly be Stahl's. Perhaps he picked up this piece of candy and put it back in the box."

"I thought of that. I found some letters of his, though, and saved them. I suppose one could get impressions of his fingers from them—to make sure."

"I have apparatus here for examining prints, Arnhardt. Let me have these things. We'll have proof then."

"All right," it seemed dragged from his throat, "I will. Anything's better than this damned uncertainty.

"It may be that the prints will prove not to be those of the person you suspect."

Arnhardt straightened suddenly and one of his hands (warm iron-hard bone and flesh) touched Rennert's on the stone bench.

"What makes you think," he asked, "that I suspect anyone?"

"Because," Rennert answered him evenly, "if you had not suspected someone very strongly—someone whom you are afraid is guilty—you wouldn't have hesitated so long about having those fingerprints examined."

The hand drew away from his.

"You're right. I did—I do—suspect a certain person. If it had stopped with Stahl's death I probably would never have said anything. But now—this can't go on! Falter and Miguel, with myself probably next!"

"Yourself?"

"Yes, can't you see that it's hitting everyone connected with the hacienda?"

The thought darted into Rennert's mind: *I wonder if that is why Solier did not want to come down. On account of fear that he would meet Stahl's fate.* He said: "Falter suspects Stephen Tolman."

He could hear Arnhardt's labored breathing. "And not me?"

"To be frank, he suspects both of you."

"Did he tell you why he suspects Tolman?"

"He thinks he may be holding a grudge against him on account of a misunderstanding in San Antonio."

"And," Arnhardt said miserably, "I wouldn't blame Tolman if he did. You know about it?"

"Only what Falter told me. Embezzlement, he said."

"That's his version, of course. I've never been able to find out how far he—and my stepfather—were involved in it. There was something wrong with the books of one of the land companies they were sponsoring. I don't know the details but some of the stockholders got suspicious and demanded an investigation. Tolman got the blame. Solier was president of the company. He didn't press any charges. Just shipped Tolman off down here. It looked to me as if he didn't want too much light thrown on the matter and so used him as a scapegoat."

"You got this version of the story from Tolman?"

"Well, no," Arnhardt hesitated, "from Ann—Mrs. Tolman."

Rennert remembered the unaccustomed softness on Arnhardt's face as he had gazed across the dinner-table at Ann Tolman's burnished hair and indulged in private speculation as to the real reason for the young man's reluctance in the matter of the fingerprints.

"Suppose," he said, "you give me those caramels and letters of Stahl's now. I shall compare the prints the first chance I get."

"All right." Arnhardt heaved himself to his feet.

They came into the patio and turned to the left. He threw open his door and fumbled for the light.

"Come in," he said as its weak illumination bathed the room.

Rennert watched him as he went to a wardrobe trunk in the corner, unlocked it and swung it open.

"Here it is," he turned with the box in his hands.

Rennert took it and with careful fingers removed the lid and a thin sheet of waxed paper. Underneath were packed firmly three rows of light brown caramels. At one end of the center row were two empty spaces. He held the box to the light and looked at the next piece. It was slightly misshapen. He fixed the lid in place again.

"And here," Arnhardt had gone back to the trunk, "are those letters of Stahl's." He gave Rennert a thick manila envelope, sealed, and watched him as he put it into a pocket. "You'll want to get fingerprints of everyone here, of course."

"Yes, that can easily be done. Since you are being so helpful we might start by taking yours."

"Mine?" Arnhardt frowned. "Why mine? You know they aren't the ones on that caramel."

Rennert noted the young man's reaction to his words. It was, he had always found, an interesting and infallible index to the human ego—this implicit assumption of one's own immunity from ordeals imposed so readily on others. As such, he discounted its importance.

"There are other objects to be considered besides the caramel," he said equably.

"With fingerprints on them?"

"Yes."

Arnhardt's rather heavy lips drew together in a hard straight line to break in a moment into a wry smile.

"All right, I haven't any objection. How's it done?"

"That will serve." Rennert nodded toward the table, where stood a bottle of ink.

"Well, this is a novel experience for me," Arnhardt said as he strode to the table and uncorked the bottle. He laughed. "I'd like to be present when you tell Miss Fahn you want to take her finger-prints. I imagine she'll take to the idea like the proverbial cat to water."

Rennert said as he laid two sheets of paper flat upon the table: "Miss Fahn probably won't know when her prints are obtained."

He took Arnhardt's right hand, daubed the fingers lightly with ink from the cork and pressed them upon the paper. First the four fingers, then the thumb. He did the same with the left hand, smiled and folded the sheets.

"Thank you, Mr. Arnhardt."

"You'll let me know as soon as you find out about those caramels?"

"Yes, as soon as

Feet scraped harshly on the paving-stones outside and the rap-ping on the door was sharp and imperative.

Arnhardt stepped forward and opened it.

Bertha Fahn stood on the threshold. Her face was coarse gray parchment and her eyes seemed to bulge behind the thick lenses of the spectacles.

"Will you please come, Mr. Arnhardt. Miguel has just died."

Arnhardt's eyes went swiftly to Rennert's face.

"Excuse me, will you, Rennert?" He jammed his hands in his pockets and accompanied the woman into the patio.

Her voice came back to Rennert's ears, smothered by the air and by the billows of fragrance: "I went in to see if there was any-thing I could do for him. He had just died. Maria wouldn't talk to me. I don't know whether she understood what I said or not—"

Rennert's mood, as he left the room, was a fatalistic one that held at the same time the dregs of bitterness. Miguel had died, as he had known he would die. Just as (the odor of the frangipani flowers was too sweet, clogging his nostrils) he knew that Falter would die before the night was over. Unless far off in San Antonio—

He started toward his room, glanced at the lighted door of the dining room and directed his steps in that direction.

He found, as he had hoped, the table still partially uncleared. The water tumblers still stood as they had been left when the meal was terminated so abruptly by Falter's fall.

From a ledge he took a lacquered Uruapan tray and, handkerchief in hand, began to place the glasses upon it. Keeping in mind the arrangement at dinner he wrote upon slips of paper the names of the persons to whom they appertained and slipped them underneath.

Lee came in before he had finished. He smiled blandly and seemed to have no curiosity at all as to Rennert's actions.

"You have plenty of glasses, Lee?"

"Yes, boss, plenty glasses."

"I'm going to take these to my room then. I'll return them in the morning."

"All light, boss," with a sound that must have been a chuckle. "Won't have to wash 'em then."

"By the way, Lee," Rennert picked up the tray, "you have entire charge of the kitchen, I believe?"

"Yes, do all work. Work all time." The Chinaman shook his head resignedly as he began piling dishes recklessly one upon another.

"Do any of the people here ever bother you by visiting the kitchen?"

Lee gave a quick sideways jerk to his head and looked up at him.

"Goddamn women," he said with emphasis.

"What women?" Rennert persisted.

"Old Mexican woman, she come out and cook leaves, make tortillas. I have to wash her dishes. Smell like hell. Miss Fahn, too, she big pain light here," emphatically he rubbed his flat paunch. "She all time monkeying around. I tell her go to hell."

"I wish, Lee, that you would keep everyone out of the kitchen for a day or two. If anyone insists on coming in, let me know." He took a coin from his pocket and flipped it to the table.

Lee pocketed it swiftly.

"All light, boss, I tell you. You give Miss Fahn kick in pants, yes?"

"Well," Rennert smiled at the vision this evoked, "I won't guarantee to do exactly that. Has Maria brought any dishes in this evening?"

"Yes, old bowl she feed Miguel with."

"I'd like to get that too."

For the first time a questioning look came into Lee's eyes.

"You want to take all dishes?" he asked.

"No, just these glasses and Maria's bowl." Rennert accompanied him into the kitchen. "Show me the bowl and I'll pick it up."

"There it is," pointing to a low pottery bowl on a cluttered table.

With his handkerchief Rennert picked it up and put it beside the glasses on the tray.

"By the way," he said as he started back into the dining room, "you might give me that glass over there on the shelf."

Lee placed the glass on the tray and followed him out. His face was suddenly convulsed with inner mirth.

"You dlink some of Mistah Falter's whisky, eh?" he asked.

"No," Rennert assured him with a smile, "I'm cold sober."

Lee shook his head.

"Think you dlink some, yes. It make you clazy too."

16
THE PATH OF STORM

RENNERT SET THE wave-band switch to the section of the dial in which was the frequency of the San Antonio station and moved the dial slowly back and forth until a voice, almost unrecognizable as that of Solier, was calling out of the crackling and spluttering of increased static: "Station W10XAKI, San Antonio, calling station XADY, Mexico. Station W10XAKI, San—"

He turned the tone control quickly to "deep" and moved to the transmitter.

"Station XADY, Mexico, answering station W10XAKI, San Antonio."

"That you, Rennert?"

"Yes, Mr. Solier."

"This static is hell, isn't it?"

"The description is mild."

"What's the news? How's Falter?"

"No better. Did you get in touch with a doctor?"

"I haven't been able to find one who's willing to undertake the trip down there."

"You inquired about any poisoning of which yellow vision is a symptom?"

"Yes. I couldn't find anyone who ever heard of it. How's Miguel Montemayor?"

"He died a few minutes ago."

"He did! Terrible! You think then that Falter—hasn't much chance?"

"Very little, I'm afraid."

"Do you know anything more about what the trouble is?"

"Not yet. I was sure that some doctor there would give us a lead on that."

Rennert wondered if the static were entirely responsible for the nervous agitation in Solier's voice: "No. No one that I've talked to so far." A pause. He thought that Solier had gone. Then the word leaped at him: "Rennert?"

"Yes?"

"Tell me frankly what's on your mind, man. Do you think those men were poisoned accidentally?"

"Frankly, Mr. Solier, I do not. I think they were deliberately poisoned—as George Stahl was poisoned two weeks ago."

"Stahl, too? Good God, Rennert, that doesn't seem possible. Still, I suppose it is the natural supposition. Have you found out yet just how they were given the stuff?"

"I think it was given to Miguel in some whisky which was in a bottle in one of the rooms."

"Which room?"

"The room which Mark Arnhardt had been occupying."

"Mark Arnhardt?"

"Yes, the room on the east side, next to the *sala*. Arnhardt has been living in it since you left. Falter had Miguel move Arnhardt's things out this afternoon so that I could move in. Those were your instructions, I believe?"

"Yes."

"My theory is that Miguel saw the whisky bottle there and drank out of it."

"What does Arnhardt say?"

"That the bottle was there when he moved in. He says he never touched it."

"Do you believe his story?"

"It sounded straightforward enough. I'm reserving judgment."

"That leaves Arnhardt in charge down there, doesn't it?"

"Yes."

"Is he cooperating with you?"

"Yes, he is convinced now that his stepfather's death is linked up with Miguel and Falter's case. He has, I think, given me some information about the circumstances of Stahl's death that will prove a material aid in clearing up the case."

"Bringing Stahl's death into it puts a new aspect on things, doesn't it?"

"It does."

"Does Arnhardt suspect anyone in particular?" Rennert hesitated.

"Yes, he does. He hasn't as yet mentioned the name, however."

Another long racking pause.

"Rennert?"

"Yes?"

"I'm worried as hell about things down there. I think I ought to be on the ground. I don't like the idea of Arnhardt being in control. I'm coming down there in the morning. By plane. I'll start at daylight. Expect me by the middle of the morning at the latest."

"I'll be glad of your assistance, Mr. Solier. You will bring a doctor if possible?"

"Yes, even if I have to kidnap one."

"The weather conditions are rather unsettled here, Mr. Solier."

"They are? What's it doing?"

"Clouds coming up from the southwest. Moving, according to radio reports, in a northeast direction. One of those circular movements in a hurricane that it's hard to tell about. It's the same storm that hit Tampico this evening." *In a northeast direction.* That meant that unless there were some unpredictable deflection in the storm's course the hacienda lay directly in its path. If (the fear had been present all evening in the back of his mind) it were to interfere with their communication . . .

"Well," Solier didn't seem greatly worried, "I'll see what report they have at the airport in the morning. The mountains will probably break the storm up during the night. Anything else now, Rennert? It's time for our stations to go off the air now."

"Nothing at present, Mr. Solier."

"Well, then, good night."

"Good night."

17
AN EMPTY HOLSTER

RENNART WALKED to his room, his ears still ringing with the din of static. While speaking with Solier an unpleasant thought had obtruded itself into his mind. It concerned the whisky which he was sure Miguel had drunk while preparing the room for his arrival. The whisky which was to have stood so temptingly before his eyes when he entered, hot, dusty, and thirsty from his trip. His eyes narrowed in speculation. It became important to find out how many people at the hacienda knew that he was to occupy that room. . . .

He locked the door and ran his eyes over the laden tray. His lips puckered in a soundless whistle as he set beside it the box of caramels, Stahl's letters, the envelope containing the tablets from Falter's desk, the water bottle and the empty whisky flask. From a suitcase he took an aluminum container, and from it a vial of black powder, a small camel's-hair brush and a magnifying lens.

He lit a cigarette and set to work.

It must have been an hour later that he leaned back in his chair and stared at the table top. His eyes ached from the strain to which they had been subjected and the tray beside him was covered with cigarette stubs.

The glasses and the pottery bowl were arrayed before him, each holding down a slip of paper. The letters were in the same row. Pushed aside to his left were the water and the whisky bottles. These were not causing the frown that cut into his forehead, however. It was the piece of caramel that lay carefully dissected upon a sheet of paper. He had just gone over the prints for the fourth time, counting ridges, classifying them into spirals and whorls, and comparing them painstakingly with those on the glasses, the bottles, the letters and the bowl. His collection was complete: Falter, Arnhardt, Stephen and Ann Tolman, Bertha Fahn, Flores, Miguel and Maria (the prints of both had been on the bowl), Lee.

He lit another cigarette, made a grimace of distaste from surfeit and stared through the haze of smoke at the result. The expression on his face was one of perplexity. Something, he had told himself at first, was wrong. Now he knew that nothing could be wrong. Although not skilled in fingerprint classification he knew that the evidence before him was, as he had told Arnhardt, incontrovertible. He was, for the moment, at a loss as to how to proceed. He found himself on the verge of indulging in fantastic explanations of the prints which he had found on the caramels.

He got up and placed the various objects carefully in the suitcase. The water bottle, being too large for this, he put in the bottom of the wardrobe. He set the suitcase beside it, locked the wardrobe, switched off the light and walked into the darkness that had blanketed the patio with the disconcerting suddenness of tropical latitudes.

The mingled aroma of flowers engulfed him, enervating as clouds of incense.

Ann Tolman was leaning against the side of the open door of Falter's office, staring out into the patio.

"How is he?" Rennert asked as he came up.

"Resting a little, I think. At least he seems to be." Her voice was lifeless.

"Has he quit talking about the yellowness of things?"

"Yes, that seems to have passed now." She put a hand up to her forehead. "I feel so helpless, not knowing what to do."

"None of us know, Mrs. Tolman."

"If you will give me a cigarette," she said, "I'll go out in the patio and smoke. It's so close in here that I'm getting a headache."

The flare of the match as Rennert held it showed the white tube vacillating between her lips. They strolled side by side to the fountain and rested on its edge.

She said nothing for a time but kept her gaze fixed over the tip of the cigarette.

"You have been very kind to me, Mr. Rennert." She spoke with sudden decision.

"About this afternoon?"

"Yes, not pressing me for an explanation."

"It was none of my concern, you know. I have the ordinary amount of curiosity but no more, I trust."

"Yet you know what I started to do?"

"Yes."

"I would have denied it, of course, if you had told. But Steve, my husband, would have known it was true. I think he suspects, as it is. Since you kept still I feel as if I should tell you."

"As you wish."

"I suppose you think that suicide is cowardly—like most people who have never been tempted to solve things that way?"

"I believe that is a question which every individual must solve for himself, Mrs. Tolman. In your case, I think that the form of suicide you contemplated took a great deal more courage than living, unless living is a very terrible burden for you."

She was silent for a long time, drawing avidly upon the cigarette.

"It has been a terrible burden for a long time. I've been able to bear it, though, until lately. It has been the heat the last week—and the deadly monotony of just existing, with no purpose at all, with no hope. I've thought sometimes that I would go mad, just for want of someone to talk to about it, someone who might suggest a way out."

Her voice was unrecognizable, so charged was it with intensity. Rennert knew that she was scarcely aware of his identity, that he was serving simply as a channel along which her pent-up emotions could flow. Wisely he kept silent.

"Steve is a consumptive. I suppose you know that. Neither of us has any money. The doctors told him that he had to go to a drier climate. We borrowed enough to get to Texas. Steve got a job with this company of Solier, Falter, and Stahl, keeping books. Things were going along well for us, we were saving up a little money and

Steve was feeling better. Then," she stopped, caught hold of herself and went on, "they said that Steve had been stealing money from the company. Mr. Solier seemed very kind about it, said they wouldn't have him arrested since they knew how badly he needed the money. He said they would send him down here to draw up plans for a hotel. They had found out that he had had training as an architect, you see."

With a quick movement she drew the cigarette from her lips and flicked ashes into the night. Her voice was unsteady with anger.

"Mr. Rennert, I know you are working for these men. I don't care. They are dishonest. Steve didn't take that money and they knew it. They just shipped him off down here so that everyone would think he was guilty and there wouldn't be any investigation. They were dishonest in this hotel business, too. They knew all the time the highway wasn't coming through here. They just put out all that fine prospectus to get people's money. I was thinking tonight, while I was in Mr. Falter's room, that in his place I'd be afraid to die—if there is another life beyond the grave."

"And yet you have been wearing yourself out nursing him."

"I suppose it isn't consistent with my feeling but I couldn't see anyone suffer without doing something to relieve him—no matter who he is."

She let the cigarette fall and ground it with her shoe. With its extinguishing some of her energy seemed to go. Her voice was suddenly weary.

"This morning Steve and I talked things over. The summer rains are coming, you know, and he must get away. He thinks that if he could get to Santa Fe, up in New Mexico, he could find some work building cottages for people who go there to write. But there's not money enough for both of us to get there. I have a little life insurance. This afternoon an idea came to me all of a sudden. If I were to die—by accident—Steve would get that money and could make another start. I tried to sleep after that but I couldn't. It was so hot, just as if a storm were brewing. I walked out into the patio then and—saw the snake." A shudder went through her. "I thought that would be the easiest way. No one would ever suspect that it wasn't an accident. If you hadn't come along everything would be settled now."

She spoke without emotion, as if it were a simple statement of an inevitable turn of events.

Rennert said quietly: "I was right, Mrs. Tolman. There was no cowardice in what you contemplated doing. I respect you for it."

She rose and said in a flat voice: "Thanks. Don't go on, though. There's nothing more to say."

They walked toward the lighted doorway.

"I noticed," Rennert said, "that you did not include Mark Arnhardt among the others associated in this company when you accused them of dishonesty."

She stopped short.

"No, he had nothing whatever to do with it," her tone was quickly defensive. "It was Solier and Falter and Mark's stepfather, Mr. Stahl. Why, it has only been in the last few weeks that Mark has even had any interest in the company. Oh, but what's the use of talking about him?"

She turned and walked rapidly to the door. When Rennert got there she was disappearing into Falter's bedroom.

He went to the desk, pulled open the upper drawer and took from it the pasteboard box. If, as he believed, these tablets had been the means of poisoning Falter, it would be dangerous to leave them there. He slipped them into a pocket and started to close the drawer. As he did so his eyes fell on the holster. He jerked the drawer further open so that the light fell full upon it.

The holster was empty.

"What's the matter?" Ann Tolman had come back into the room and must have seen the grim look on his face.

He closed the drawer and walked around the table to her.

"I told you, Mrs. Tolman, that I admired your courage this afternoon. This isn't the way, however. It's utter folly, from any viewpoint you wish. If it is judged suicide your husband will not benefit by the insurance money. If it passes as murder someone else will suffer."

She stared at him, a puzzled frown on her face. "What do you mean?"

"When I was in this room last there was a pistol in that drawer. It's not there now."

"Oh!" she raised a hand slowly to her throat. "And you think that I— But I didn't!" She looked him straight in the eyes. "I give you my word I didn't take it. I didn't even know it was there."

For a long moment their eyes held.

"Do you believe me?" she asked.

Rennert nodded.

"Yes, Mrs. Tolman, I believe you." He glanced at the closed bedroom door. "You were in there several times tonight, I suppose?"

"Yes, every few minutes."

"With the door closed?"

"Either closed or partly so. I didn't want any noises to disturb him."

"Did you hear anyone enter this room?"

"Yes, I did," she said hastily. "Someone came in while I was in the bedroom. About an hour ago, it was. I supposed it was someone wanting to ask about Mr. Fatter. When I came out in a few minutes there was no one here." The color drained slowly from her face. "It must have been someone who wanted that gun—"

"Obviously it was someone who wanted that gun very badly."

Rennert went through the patio again, walking with lagging steps. He stopped in front of the door of the *sala*, where he had watched the green worm crawl toward the yellow marigolds.

The elusive memory that he sought had come closest down the labyrinth of thought at that moment. He felt that there was need— imperative need—for haste in its capture now that behind one of these doors there was a loaded gun.

That doctor on the train had been talking about his work in a little town along the Gulf. About the terrible fatality among native children—

Then it clicked and he knew how Stahl and Miguel had died, how Tilghman Falter was dying, slowly, irremediably.

He turned and went into the *sala*. He switched on the radio and for twenty minutes, regardless of assigned hours of broadcast, called Solier's San Antonio station.

Static was his only answer.

Finally he gave it up. Cold realization came in a douche. His call had been an SOS with a man's life the forfeit. Now until daylight the hacienda was shut off from communication, the knowledge that he had gained of little use in the face of his helplessness to stay further attacks.

And the worst of it was that he had no idea from what quarter they were coming.

18
HIBISCUS

BERTHA FAHN CLOSED her door and groped through the darkness for the light switch. She found it, pressed it and stood very still in the center of the room, telling herself that she must not give way to the feeling of panic that was beginning to surge through her.

She always felt it when she watched the darkness closing in on her, heavy, almost palpable, emphasized by the stars that hung such an incalculable distance away. Tonight it was worse. There were no stars. Across the courtyard one man lay dead and another, perhaps, dying. A little shiver went through her at the recollection of the way Mr. Falter had stared at her over the dinner table, of the way he had fallen forward, his hand overturning the white carnations.

She made her decision quickly, had made it really before she came into the room. She would leave the hacienda the next day. Now that her work was almost completed there was nothing to keep her in this place which at first had seemed so beautifully to embody the romantic. She wanted to see long vistas of electric lights again, to feel pavement under her feet, and about her the reassuring surge of the city.

She stared at the blackness framed by the window, wishing that there were blinds. A person could stand out there in the night and watch her—

Resolutely she put that thought out of her mind. If she were going to leave in the morning she would have to finish as much of her task as possible tonight, prepare everything so that there would be no chance of a slip-up at the border. She had worked so hard these long hot days that the thought of a last-minute discovery was unbearable. Long ago she had faced and conquered conscientiously the ethical problem of what she was doing. Science (the word always stood before her capitalized) was greater than man, existing without his creation. Its servants were (or ought to be) beyond the petty restrictions of laymen. The researcher in his laboratory, for example, experimenting with guinea pigs . . .

She went to the scarred wardrobe trunk in the corner and pushed it open. She took from about her throat a thin gold chain to which was attached a small key. She inserted this in the lock of the lower compartment and drew out a deep tray.

She carried it to the table under the electric bulb and put it down beside the solitary hibiscus flower that raised its red petals out of a thin vase of blue Jalisco glass. She picked up the topmost of three heavy albums and laid it on the top of the table. From a drawer she took a stick of wax, a candle and a packet of matches.

She sat down and opened the album flat upon the table. At her left hand she put a little stack of transparent glazed envelopes and at her right a neat pile of postcards. She eyed the postcards and frowned. There wouldn't be enough, just as she had calculated. She would have to ask Mr. Rennert for those which he had brought.

She started to get up, hesitated, and looked at her watch. Surely he wouldn't be going to bed so early. Still, he had had a long trip that day and would doubtless be tired. On the other hand, being from the city, he would be accustomed to late hours. She got up. But men here in the tropics lounged about in their rooms with such a disregard for clothing. Once when she had gone into Mr. Falter's office he had been lying in the bedroom, with the door open! Hastily she sat down again, solving her dilemma by postponing its solution.

Carefully opening one of the envelopes she took out a dried flower. It was a small thing, with four dark brown petals that looked now like withered skin. One brown leaf still clung to the short stalk.

She laid it flat upon one oblong section of the blank album. She took one of the postcards and applied the tip of the piece of wax to the flame of the candle. When it had begun to melt she applied the end to four places near the edges of the reverse side of the card. She inserted the corners of the card into the slits designed for them and pressed down. She raised her hand in a moment, then passed her fingers lightly over the surface. It was held firmly in place. Under its smoothness no one could feel (unless after extremely careful examination) any protuberance to show that the flower was there.

It was, she thought, an admirable idea of hers, one that would enable her to carry back some of the fruits of her labors. . . .

She worked on, her fingers growing more nimble with repetition.

These flowers, sought after in the recesses of the rocks, along drying *arroyo* beds, had taken on personalities for her. Each recalled the event of its discovery, when it had given up the long game of hide-and-seek and had let her find it.

The last of the postcards was in place and she sat in a sort of reverie, her eyes on the red hibiscus. Hibiscus. The syllables still retained their power to evoke for her visions of hot sensuous beauty and to send warm stirrings of the blood through her tired old body. Just as they had done when she was a gawky timid girl peopling her loneliness with beings from the pages of fiction. Somehow it had always been the flowers that kept lines as vivid before her eyes as the day she had first read them. She let her eyes close and saw one scene again. A shipwreck and surf pounding against a coral beach somewhere. Polynesia? Torres Strait? Sandalwood? It didn't matter. "The tropic sun beat down, spreading a glitter as of diamonds over the beach. In the drowsy palm trees purple and green parrots chattered noisily. Terence Holderness dragged himself out of reach of the angry waves and lay upon the sand, his bronzed muscular chest rising and falling under a tattered shirt. He, a shipwrecked wanderer, while his unscrupulous brother, the baronet that he should have been, rode foxes at Cranston Castle! He opened his eyes and saw a native girl standing before him. A sarong encircled her graceful body and in her black hair was a hibiscus flower—"

She realized suddenly that the sound in her ears wasn't the surf on a coral beach but a gently insistent rapping at her door.

After a momentary debate as to whether or not to answer it she decided that whoever it was undoubtedly had seen the light under her door. Hastily closing the album she laid it and the remaining envelopes and the wax in the tray. She blew out the candle and went to the door.

It was Mr. Rennert. The uncertain light gave his face a stern appearance. Almost, she thought, formidable.

"Come in," she said.

19
PLASTIC WAX

HE STEPPED into the room and she closed the door behind him. She gestured toward a chair and as he sat down resumed her seat by the table. It gave her confidence in herself—this rigid posture in the hard straight chair, with books and papers ranged before her in curt business-like fashion. It was a safeguard of a sort against the vaguely disturbing effects of contact with masculinity which made her feel ill at ease.

She picked up a fountain pen and held it upright, like a proud masthead, as she said: "What can I do for you, Mr. Rennert?" It sounded, she knew, unbearably prim, so she added colorlessly: "Or is this just a social call?"

Suddenly she remembered their encounter under the frangi-pani tree, when he had surprised her in such a foolish attitude, with her face buried in that flower. It was another vision which the frangipani had brought to her with its smell—a scene from a novel by a lady writer whose works had been frowned upon by her parents. She wondered, angrily, if he had known that she had al-most blushed and what he had thought of her as she chattered on inanely about the blood-tree of Yuquane to cover up her agitation.

His smile was pleasant but she had the feeling that his clear brown eyes were studying her closely.

"There is nothing to be done for Miguel or Maria tonight," he said. "A doctor should be here in the morning."

"I'm so sorry about Miguel's death." She spoke with genuine feeling, wishing that she could forget the stolid-faced woman who

107

had crouched beside the bed and stared with dry reproachful eyes at the little Virgin upon the wall.

A pungent scorching smell stung her nostrils. Hastily putting out a hand to the tray, where the hot wax must have come into contact with something, she took out the albums and envelopes and cards. The wax slid further down. She had to lay the things upon the table in order to retrieve it. She dropped it beside the candle and bent over her treasures.

Apparently no damage had been done. The wax had touched only the edges of some of the envelopes. She started to put them back into the tray and remembered the man who sat a few feet away from her, remembered with a stab of alarm what Mr. Falter had said about him the day before. That he was a Treasury Department agent, one of those alert-eyed men who kept a watch at the border—

In confusion she looked at him, saw that his eyes, before they rose to meet hers, had been fixed on the albums and the envelopes.

"Oh, pardon me," she laughed forcedly. "I was afraid that some of my things were being damaged."

"Quite all right, Miss Fahn." His tone seemed to her too conversational, as if he were trying to hide his suspicion.

Her fingers were unsteady as she arranged the things in the tray and carried it to the trunk.

"Let me help you." He started to get up.

"No, no," she said hastily. "I can carry it."

As she came back he was straightening up in his chair, the light bringing out the silver on his temples. In his hand he held a dried pressed flower.

Neither of them spoke for what seemed to her an endless time.

"I believe," he said as he laid the flower upon the table, "that you dropped this."

"Yes," she spoke faintly, "I believe I did."

She took it and carried it back to the trunk, where she let it fall into the tray. She sat down and picked up the pen out of sheer necessity for something to break the tension that she felt in the room.

"I'm rather nervous tonight," she said. "I'm getting ready to leave tomorrow."

"Oh." There was just a tinge of surprise to his voice. "I didn't know that."

"I've just made up my mind," she hastened to explain. "I've finished everything that I had to do here and would like to get home as quickly as possible."

"In that case I suppose I have arrived too late with your postcards." He put a hand into his pocket and brought out a pack. "I don't know whether I picked out the views that you wanted," he said, laying them on the table. "I got some of them in San Antonio, with pictures of the Alamo and the Missions, and some in Monterrey—the Cathedral, the Obispado—"

"Oh, it doesn't matter," she interrupted, "about the views. Any kind will do. Thank you so much. I can still use them."

There was silence for a moment. It was, she thought, a peculiarly in-pressing sort of silence, from which even the ordinary little noises from outside seemed excluded. It made her distinctly restive, as if there were a personal menacing quality to it.

Mr. Rennert, evidently, felt nothing of this, for he was going on in his pleasantly modulated voice: "In view of your departure, Miss Fahn, I had better bring up a matter that I had intended to postpone until we got better acquainted. It's about your shares in the company which owns this hacienda. Mr. Solier has commissioned me to make you another offer for them. He is willing to pay—"

"Oh, it doesn't make any difference," her voice rang oddly strained and unnatural in her ears.

"I am to understand then that you are not willing to consider any offer?"

"What?"

He repeated his words.

"Oh, yes. I meant that I was ready to sell the shares. They're in a safety-deposit box in San Antonio. I'll give them to Mr. Solier when I go through there."

"Very well, Miss Fahn." She wondered if there had been, just for an instant, a speculative look in his eyes. "And now, if you will sign a release for them I'll give you Mr. Solier's check and everything will be in shape."

"All right. What do I sign?"

He took a paper from his pocket and laid it before her, together with an uncapped fountain pen.

She glanced over it hastily and tried to keep her hand steady as she affixed her signature to the bottom.

"Good," he said as she handed it back to him. "And here is your check. It is made out for the amount you paid for the shares. That is right, isn't it?"

"Yes." She scarcely glanced at it as he put it on one corner of the desk. She took out her handkerchief and, regardless of delicacy, touched her forehead with it. How, she wondered, could he maintain such cool composure in that stifling hot room? "I wonder if you would mind opening the door, Mr. Rennert? This room is so close."

He got up and complied. As he returned to his chair he asked with what seemed to her a great deal of solicitude: "Aren't you feeling well, Miss Fahn?"

"Oh, it's only the heat. I'm sure that we are going to have a storm. I have been expecting it all evening. I don't see why Mr. Flores couldn't have warned us. Not, of course, that it would have done any good."

"I beg your pardon, Miss Fahn?"

"Why, there's no place to go to get away from it. We would just have to sit here anyway and wait for it to come. Back in Austin we have an old-fashioned storm cellar. But here—"

"I meant about Mr. Flores. How would he be able to give warning of an approaching storm?"

"Oh," her voice hovered for a moment on vagueness, "I don't know that he could have, of course, but it's possible, I should think. I don't see any reason for being an astronomer if one can't predict storms, do you?"

"I didn't know that Mr. Flores was an astronomer?"

"Yes, I'm sure he is. At least he carries a telescope about with him."

"A telescope?"

"Yes, I've seen him with it several times out in the mountains, while I was collecting specimens."

"Can you describe the telescope to me, Miss Fahn?"

She wondered why he was so persistent in the matter of the telescope but grasped at it as another topic of conversation, lags in which always disconcerted her.

"I was never close enough to see it very plainly, of course. Just a small metal telescope on a tripod. The only time I got near him he saw me coming and put it away in that black case. What he needs the spade for, I don't know. He always carries one with him when he goes out."

"Have you ever seen him digging with the spade?"

"No, every time I've seen him the spade has been lying on the ground and he has been watching the telescope. I don't think he wants it mentioned for some reason. I said something about it to him one day. He just glared at me. Since then I've never felt like asking him about the weather."

Surely, she thought, that was enough about the dapper Mr. Flores, of whom she had an opinion that was perhaps unwarranted. Her eyes rested on the pack of postcards awaiting her attention. Mr. Rennert was a most pleasant man, she had decided, although a bit unpredictable in his interests. If the time were longer she was sure that his company would prove to be very agreeable about the hacienda, particularly at the dinner-table, where it was so difficult to keep things going smoothly. She was sure that he would prove to be less coarse than Mr. Falter, less brusque than Mr. Arnhardt, and more communicative than Mr. Tolman, who would get spells when he simply sat and stared at a blank wall. Still, she must fill that last album tonight.

She wondered if he had read her thoughts because he said: "I wonder, Miss Fahn, if you have some manual here that would give me information about the botany of this section of Mexico?"

"I am afraid that very little knowledge has ever been made available before," she stressed the word gently, "on the subject. There have been a few scattered monographs, mostly in Spanish and very incomplete."

"And now?"

She tried to make her smile properly diffident.

"I have just finished my doctor's dissertation on the flora of Northern Mexico. I have it here."

"Really, I hadn't expected this." There seemed to be genuine enthusiasm in his voice. "Would it be too great a favor to ask you to let me glance over it tonight? I shall promise to return it the first thing in the morning."

"Well," she hesitated, "I might let you have the carbon copy."

"That will be very kind of you."

She opened a drawer of the table, took out a bulky manuscript wrapped in brown paper and handed it to him.

"Thank you very much," he took it and stood up. "And now I won't bother you any more tonight."

She rose and smiled. After all, it was foolish to have felt any alarm over those albums. The gray that touched his thin brown hair at the temples was, she felt, almost a bond between them, betraying as it did the relentless approach of old age.

"It has been altogether a pleasure, Mr. Rennert. If there is any information I can give you about the plants, you must let me know."

"I shall probably do that, Miss Fahn. Good night."

"Good night, Mr. Rennert."

She sat down at the table and listened to the sound of his feet die away on the stones. Somewhat to her surprise she realized, now that he had gone, how pleasurable a sort of excitement she had derived from his visit. She gazed for a moment at the chair into which his body had fitted so compactly. If there should happen to be any trouble at the border she might even be able to turn to him for assistance.

As she went over to the trunk for the albums she began to wonder what he had wanted with her dissertation. One wouldn't have expected a man of the world, such as he obviously was, to be interested in plants and flowers.

20
MISS FAHN IS FRIGHTENED

". . . AN INDIGENOUS perennial plant," Rennert re-read the lines, "with an herbaceous, erect, branching, furrowed stem, which rises from two to five feet in height. The leaves are alternate or scattered, sessile, oblong lanceolate, attenuated at both ends, sinuated and toothed on the margin, conspicuously veined, of a yellowish-green color, and dotted on their under surface. The flowers are very numerous, small, of the same color with the leaves, and arranged in long, leafless, terminal panicles, which are composed of slender, dense, glomerate, alternating spikes."

He inserted the sheet of yellow copy paper in its place in Bertha Fahn's work on "The Flora of Northern Mexico," lit a cigarette and rested his head on the back of the chair.

He stared thoughtfully at a gray moth that had sailed out of the night to beat frantic wings against the unshaded light bulb.

What he had just read offered, he knew, a possibility that it would not do to neglect. In view of the knowledge that he had acquired in the last few hours he had almost discarded his first theory—that the dark soil about the hacienda had lifted the means of destruction toward a calculating murderer's hand. Now (his eyes followed the erratic course of the moth) he was faced with that theory again. And the inference that of the individuals under that roof only two—both of them women—possessed sufficient knowledge to look for and find in the patio itself or in the sparse vegetation of those rocky slopes certain yellowish-green flowers arranged (What was that description?) in "long, leafless, terminal panicles."

113

So absorbed was he in the unpleasant implications of this train of thought that his cigarette fell from his fingers when a woman's scream, scaling into a high, terror-filled note, cut through the enveloping stillness.

The patio was impossibly still in the reflux of the scream, oppressed by the black lid of the sky, as he ran along the stones toward the light that flooded from the open door next to his.

The scene inside halted him by its unexpectedness. Bertha Fahn stood by the window, with a chair held protectingly before her.

In front of her was Lee, the Chinaman. He still wore the blue serge trousers and the sweater but his sleeves were rolled up, exposing thin wasted arms. In his right hand he held a long carving knife, with which he was gesticulating wildly as with his left he grasped the table. Wadded under his fingers was a white apron. He was swaying drunkenly to and fro and talking in an unintelligible singsong voice.

Rennert came up behind him, grasped his right arm and twisted. The knife clattered on the tiles.

He swung the man around. Lee lurched forward, his lips curling back over his teeth, and struck out blindly.

Rennert hit him neatly on the point of the chin. Lee fell backward, struck the edge of the table and collapsed on the floor.

"Did he hurt you, Miss Fahn?" Rennert was at her side.

She lowered the chair, moved toward the bed and sank down upon it, covering her face with her hands.

"No, no," she spoke through interlocked fingers.

Rennert glanced about the room. On a dresser he caught sight of a small flask that must contain, if he remembered his boyhood days aright, smelling salts. He walked over, uncorked it and held it to his nose. Just what, he demanded of himself with an irrepressible surge of mock gravity at the anticlimax, did one do to revive prostrated females now that smelling salts were out of date?

He sat down on the bed and extended the bottle.

"Just take a breath of this, Miss Fahn, and you'll feel better."

She took away her hands and stared for an instant blankly at the green glass. He raised it and she drew a deep breath. Her nose contracted and tears started to her eyes.

"That's better," she pushed away his hand. "Thank you." She drew out a handkerchief, removed her glasses and daubed at her eyes. In a moment she dropped the handkerchief and her gaze sought the still figure on the floor. She made an attempt to swallow.

"Now," Rennert said, "do you feel like telling me what happened?"

She looked at him.

"He just—just came in," she said unevenly. "I was there at the table working. I heard someone behind, me. I turned around and there he was. With that knife. He said something that I couldn't understand. I thought he was drunk and told him to go away. Then he started toward me, waving the knife and that apron. I screamed." She said simply, "That's all."

Rennert got up. He restrained just in time an impulse to pat her on the shoulder.

"I'll get him out of here. Don't worry. He won't bother you any more tonight."

He walked across the room and started to bend down. As he did so his eyes swept the top of the table.

The album lay open by the unflickering flame of the candle. On the right-hand side three postcards had been put into place. In the center of the lower space, sharply outlined against the dark green paper, was a dried yellowish flower.

He stared at it thoughtfully for a second or two then straightened up.

"By the way, Miss Fahn," he said, carefully casual, "I have been interested this evening in reading your dissertation. I see that you mention worm-seed, or Mexican tea, among the flora of northern Mexico. Have you ever found any specimens near by?"

She was pushing back the knot of hair that had slipped down, giving her face a grotesque appearance. She stared at him as if in incomprehension.

"*Chenopodium anthelminticum*, you mean."

"Yes, that's the scientific name for it, I believe."

She adjusted the spectacles more firmly upon the bone-bridged nose and gazed through their lenses with a slight forward movement of her head.

"No," she said, her voice normal again, "I've never seen any about here, although it does grow in parts of northern Mexico. Farther to the south, too. Mateo Battieri took specimens back to Europe from near Orizaba, unless I am mistaken, in 1850—"

"But you are certain that there are none near this hacienda?"

She nodded.

"Yes, I'm positive. I've been all over these mountains this spring and I've never seen any."

Rennert picked up Lee's body, held it lightly in his arms.

"Do you know," he asked over it, "what medicinal uses *Chenopodium anthelminticum* has?"

"It's used as a vermifuge, Mr. Rennert."

"Thank you, Miss Fahn. Good night." He started toward the door.

"Good night," came from behind him after a full six seconds.

"Want me to help you?" Stephen Tolman, clad in a dressing-gown, faced him on the threshold.

"I can carry him," Rennert said. "You might get the knife."

As he stepped into the patio he heard over the Chinaman's stertorous breathing Ann Tolman's low frightened voice: "Mr. Rennert? What has happened?

"Nothing to be alarmed about."

Before he could go on Tolman was at his side.

"Just Lee on another drunk," he said in a voice that was, Rennert felt, too light.

He made his way into the inner patio, leaving husband and wife conversing in low tones.

The door of Lee's room next to the kitchen stood ajar. He pushed it open with his foot. A dim light illuminated the interior.

He laid the man on a cot, ascertained that the blow had done him no serious injury, and stood looking about the bare quarters.

On a chair beside the cot were three unsmoked cigarettes. The stub of another had burnt itself out against the varnished wood. Two more lay crushed upon the floor.

Rennert picked up the cigarettes and examined them. They were of coarse, stringy dark fiber rolled in yellowish brown paper. He held them one by one to his nose, extracted a bit of the fiber and tasted it. He spat it out quickly. Thrusting the cigarettes into his pocket he turned off the light and left the room.

Stephen Tolman stood outside, holding the knife uncertainly.

"Want this?" he asked.

"I'll take it to my room," Rennert said. "It's a rather dangerous plaything to leave lying about."

"Expect Lee to start another rampage?"

"No, he'll sleep the rest of the night, I think."

"I came up just as you hit him. He went out like a light, didn't he? You must pack considerable of a wallop in that fist of yours." Tolman handed him the knife.

It wasn't, Rennert knew, altogether the blow that had been responsible for Lee's quick collapse, but he said nothing. They walked away together.

"I wish they wouldn't keep that damned Chinaman around here," Tolman said. "That's twice he has gone berserk."

"What happened before?"

"He went after Miss Fahn, same as tonight. Falter got him in time." Tolman hesitated. "I don't think, though, that he would actually have hurt her. He didn't have the knife. Just went to her room and yelled at her in Chinese. Ordinarily he's a peaceable enough fellow."

"Any particular reason why he should dislike Miss Fahn?"

"Well, you saw that scene in the dining room tonight."

"Yes, I surmised that it had been enacted before."

"Every day or so. I can't say that I blame him much for getting sore, the way she's always fussing at him. She goes in the kitchen and tries to tell him how to cook. She thinks that because he's a Chinaman he smokes opium and is always threatening to fire him. He says that nobody can fire him but Falter and tells her to get out. She gets mad and," he laughed drily, "there they go."

Rennert asked thoughtfully: "When did this other outburst take place?"

"Just before he left, about two weeks ago."

"About the time the water began to disappear from the kitchen, then."

"What?" Tolman stopped under the archway between the patios. Rennert repeated his words.

"Why, yes, I believe it was about that time." Tolman seemed to be intent on contemplation of the sky.

Rennert was thinking of the cigarettes which he had found in Lee's room. *I wonder*, he was asking himself, *if I am making a mistake in separating so completely the different strands in this case. If in the past they became twisted one may now lead off at a tangent which I have not suspected so far. A tangent, perhaps, that leads to murder.*

"Black as hell, isn't it?" Tolman remarked. "A storm must be coming up. What about coming into the room for a chat?"

Rennert brought his attention sharply back. "I'd be glad to," he said.

21
A FLOWER IN SILHOUETTE

As they walked through the darkness Tolman said in a voice curiously unlike his own: "You're being very kind, Mr. Rennert."

"In what way?"

"By paying me a visit. You don't know how good it is to see a new face here, to have someone new to talk to. I get awfully lonesome sometimes."

Invariably, Rennert knew, men will bare their emotions more freely in the darkness or in their correspondence, when no vis-à-vis can scrutinize their countenances for signs of self-consciousness. But this was something deeper, a note that rang with intensity. An appeal to his sympathy? Scarcely that, the man had seemed to speak to himself. He wondered if it weren't merely the familiar echo of self-commiseration carried to an extreme.

He said: "I've been intending all evening to get better acquainted but haven't had the opportunity so far."

"You *have* been busy, I know."

When they were in the room Tolman spoke with forced lightness: "Don't stumble over the bearskin rugs or the cocktail trays or the butler. I'd recommend one of those chairs there the hard straight-backed one with the cracked rung or the rocker that creaks if you dare rock."

Rennert chose the rocker.

The room was furnished more simply than his own, with what were obviously the left-overs from the other rooms. The mirror over the dresser had a crack whose presence was not dissembled by a strip of plaster. The rocker *did* creak as he found out when he shifted the weight of his body.

He proffered cigarettes. Tolman, who had shed the dressing-gown, shook his head.

"Thanks. I can't use 'em"

Rennert lit one. He didn't particularly want it but to have returned them to his pocket would have seemed too obvious a gesture of sympathy.

He surveyed with interest the man who reclined before him in the unshielded glare of the lamp. Tolman was evidently in his late twenties, although there was something about his long face, a looseness of the skin, a look of weariness in the lacklustre blue eyes, that made him seem older. His hands lay flat upon the coverlet—white, delicate hands with blue veins traced across their surfaces. The fingers were long and tapering. He rubbed their tips gently upon the cloth as he said: "Ann just told me that Falter is worse. There doesn't seem to be anything we can do, does there?"

"We can only hope that a doctor gets here before it's too late."

"Not much chance of that, is there?"

"Not much."

The fingers were moving very slowly down the thin thighs.

"What's it all about, Rennert? Falter's stroke at dinner tonight and Miguel's death?"

"I was going to ask you for your opinion, Tolman. I have been here less than twelve hours, remember."

Tolman said nothing for a full minute. He raised himself upon the pillows and stretching out his legs stared down at his bare toes.

"Rennert," he said, "do you mind if I am rather blunt?"

"Not at all."

"Well, then, where do you come in on all this? I didn't hear anything about your coming until breakfast this morning and then Falter just mentioned the fact that you were going to stay here at the hacienda for a while."

"I am here as agent for Solier. He sent me down on a business matter. That is all."

Tolman had turned his head and was looking directly at him. There was something disconcerting about the steadiness of his gaze.

"You are interested in his company?" he asked.

"Not at all. I merely know what Solier told me that a company was formed to build a hotel here, that the highway missed the place and that they were left with it on their hands."

Tolman's eyes did not waver.

"I was surprised," he said, "at the idea of your being mixed up with a bunch like Solier and Falter. You're sure you didn't put any money in the deal?"

"Not a red cent."

"Well, don't."

"Want to tell me why you said that?"

Tolman's eyes strayed at last.

"Because of what you did this afternoon," he said flatly, "for Ann." He cleared his throat. "I'd do anything in the world for the man who did that. The Solier-Falter-Stahl company is crooked, has been from the beginning. I've worked for them. I ought to know," a shade of bitterness crept into the last words.

"I understand that you drew the plans for the hotel."

"Yes, they still have me making changes in them. That's what I get my room and board for."

Rennert leaned forward.

"You say they *still* have you making changes?"

"Yes."

"But I thought the whole project had been abandoned?"

Tolman drew his knees up and clasped his hands about them.

"That's the queer part of it. I thought they had given up their idea when the road was changed. But just four days ago Falter had me make some further changes. It looks as if they were going ahead."

Rennert drew slowly upon his cigarette.

"A hopeless location for a hotel," he said to himself as much as to Tolman.

"If it is a hotel."

"What do you mean?"

Tolman raised one shoulder in a shrug.

"I don't know—and that's straight. It's just that the thought has struck me several times that the plans are the goofiest I ever saw for a hotel."

"In what way?"

"I'll show you." He leaned over and opened a drawer in the bedside table. He took out a drawing-board upon which a blueprint had been affixed with thumb tacks. "See here," he held it to the light.

Rennert got up and leaned over.

Tolman's long forefinger was running over the surface.

"You see," he said, "the building is to have three stories. The first floor and the second are the regulation hotel style. On the first, a lobby, offices, dining room and kitchen; on the second, a mezzanine floor with six suites opening off it. But," his finger came to a stop, "when we come to the top floor, what's there? One large room with a glass skylight." He looked up at Rennert. "If this is a hotel where are the guests to stay? Those half-dozen suites on the second floor wouldn't accommodate nearly enough to make the place pay."

"This is the only building?"

"Yes."

Rennert was staring thoughtfully at the section devoted to the upper floor.

"They never gave you any indication as to the purpose of that top floor?"

"None at all. They just said they didn't want it partitioned off into rooms. They insisted, too, on the glass skylight."

"Just whom do you mean by 'they'?"

"Solier gave me the first instructions in San Antonio. In a rather general way. Then he and Falter and Stahl had a meeting here at the hacienda and called me in. They were more specific then and gave the orders about the top floor and the skylight."

"And the changes that you have been making recently?"

"Falter has been instructing me about them. After conferences with Solier on the radio, I believe. They concern little details mostly."

"Don't they consult Arnhardt?"

Tolman hesitated.

"I think they disregard him mostly. You see, at the beginning he had no interest in the company. It's only since George Stahl's death that he has been a member." He seemed disposed to veer off this subject. "About that skylight and all. I've wondered sometimes if they mean it for a gigantic laboratory of some kind. Though why they should need the lay-out on the first two floors is beyond me."

Rennert felt his interest mounting. These plans and the fact that a power plant had been installed recently at the hacienda were component parts, he felt, of some element of the case that was gradually taking shape in his mind. So far he had failed to discern any motive behind these apparently purposeless crimes. But if there were more than an abandoned project for a hotel at stake . . .

"But you haven't told me," he said, "what interpretation you give to recent events here. I am referring, of course, to Miguel's death and Falter's illness."

Tolman said nothing. Rennert looked at him, trying to fathom the reason for his silence.

He had shoved the board onto the table and was lying back upon the pillows, staring out the window. A curious change had come over his face. The alertness which had marked it was gone now and in its place was the complete lack of expression of a man whose body is alone in a room and whose mind is groping slowly down some private channel of its own.

With a visible effort he brought his attention back. "Pardon me, Mr. Rennert, what was it you said?"

Rennert repeated.

"Oh." Tolman's eyes were directed toward him but he wasn't looking at him, only staring in his direction with a blank fixity. His voice was as inanimate as his face. "Well, it can't be any infectious disease, can it?"

"I think that possibility can be discarded."

"Then that leaves only one thing. Poison." Tolman let his eyelids droop as if in weariness and a hectic flush spread over his cheekbones. Rennert had the strange, and uncomfortable, feeling that he had watched something die behind those blue eyes. Something essential that left behind it only emptiness. "It gives one a terrible feeling, doesn't it, to think that some person with whom he is associated every day is a poisoner? I suppose you wonder why I'm not afraid—for Ann and myself. It's because we're harmless, don't stand in anyone's way."

"In anyone's way? I don't think I understand your meaning, Mr. Tolman."

"You see what's behind these killings, don't you?" Still that lifeless flow of words.

"What?" Rennert felt that in his directness he was cutting through a confusing, vaguely defined welter of emotions, possibly brushing aside as veiling the main issue obscurities that might be meaningful.

"Control of the hacienda. That's the only reason for doing away with Stahl and Falter and Miguel. Someone wants complete and undisturbed possession. If some men want a thing bad enough they get it. Nothing can stop them. The survival of the fittest, you know." Tolman stopped, his face working, and made a choking noise in his throat. "Sorry, Rennert," he spoke through the folds of a handkerchief clamped over his mouth, "I'd better not talk any more tonight. This damned cough."

Yet when Rennert closed the door there had been no cough.

He glanced across the patio.

Ann Tolman and Mark Arnhardt stood sharply silhouetted in the doorway of Falter's office. Her low laugh rippled across the flowers. Her hands were raised high, her bare arms slashing darkly across his white shirt front, as she fixed in his lapel a fire-red hibiscus.

22
A SHOT IN THE NIGHT

A FAINT COOLNESS had come into the air so that Rennert's perspiration-damp clothing sent a faint chill through his body, but there was no diminution of the electric tensity with which the atmosphere was charged. The sky was impenetrably black, shrouding the stars.

He went to his room and, without turning on the light, threw himself fully clothed upon the bed. He did not intend to sleep as yet and so left the door open for the sake of the draft between it and the window. There was a dull throbbing in his head and in his ears, no mistaking it now, the uncomfortable pressure upon the drums of which Miss Fahn had complained. *In this wilderness on the margin of the tropics a building with a huge glass-domed roof . . . a building that appeared a hotel but wasn't . . . a building offering enough potential gain to tempt an individual to triple murder. . . .*

The sharp crack of a pistol shot brought him to his feet.

Lights cut crisscross swathes across the patio and two voices were calling. A man's voice—Tolman's—crying desperately: "Ann! Ann! Where are you?" A woman's voice—his wife's—sharp with terror: "Mark! Are you all right? Answer me!"

As Rennert's flashlight swept the beds of flowers Arnhardt's roughened voice said: "Right here." The light sought and found him.

He was leaning against the bowl of the fountain, one hand clasping a handkerchief to his left shoulder. The handkerchief and the hand were dark with blood that glistened as it seeped between his fingers and trickled down his wrist.

He raised his head and looked from Tolman's face to Ann's, both white masks against the night, and at Rennert.

"Someone shot me," he spoke through set teeth. "It's not serious—"

"Help me," Rennert said to Tolman. "We'll take him to his room."

"I can walk." Arnhardt was quick in protest.

He stalked across the patio, Rennert following him. Tolman stood in evident indecision, then turned in the direction of his own room. Ann had vanished.

Arnhardt's door was open. As they went toward it a figure stepped out of the shelter of the eaves into the path of the torch. It was Flores. He was tying about his waist the cord of a vivid red and black dressing-gown. His eyes centered on Arnhardt and his fingers were suddenly still.

"What has happened?" he asked, a sibilance creeping into his English for the first time.

"Mr. Arnhardt has been hurt," Rennert said briefly.

"The shot awoke me. It took me several moment to realize what it was. Is he seriously injured?"

"I think not."

Rennert preceded Arnhardt into the latter's room and turned on the light. As he closed the door the Mexican was standing a few feet away, staring inside with eyes that were as fixed and unmoving as two chips of obsidian. He was running the tip of his tongue quickly and nervously over his upper lip.

Rennert turned into the room and watched Arnhardt sink into a chair, take away the handkerchief, and wring it between the fingers of his right hand. Blood squirted to the floor.

Still in silence he leaned over Arnhardt, removed his coat and, unloosening his tie, stripped away the shirt from his left shoulder.

Ann came into the room with a bowl of water and cloths.

Arnhardt stared at her, his face rigid.

"Ann," he said with a trace of brusqueness as his eyes rested on the stained tiles, "go on back. This is no place for you."

She said nothing, did not even look at him, but drew another chair forward and set the bowl upon it. She handed Rennert one of the cloths and stood still and firm-faced as he bathed the wound. The bullet, he soon saw, had plowed through the flesh of the chest just below the armpit. It was bleeding profusely and looked serious but probably was not.

In a few minutes he stood back and surveyed the impromptu bandage which he had fixed.

"I think," he said, "that will suffice for the time being."

"Thanks."

There was silence for a moment while Arnhardt stared stonily at the floor, his hands clasped about the caps of his knees.

"Excuse me now." Ann Tolman spoke for the first time. "Let me know if there's anything I can do," she looked at neither of them but gave the impression somehow that she was addressing Rennert rather than Arnhardt.

"Very well, Mrs. Tolman."

When she had gone and the door was closed Rennert propped a foot on the chair beside the other.

"Now then?" he said. "What about it?"

Arnhardt said nothing for a moment but maintained his unbudging pose. When he raised his eyes to Rennert's at last they were cold and bright with anger.

"What about it? Just this," with a downward motion of his jaw toward his wounded shoulder. "I was coming through the patio, headed for this room, when somebody used me for a little target practice. The shot came from somewhere straight ahead of me. In front of the door, I think."

"You saw no one?"

"No, it was dark."

"Were lights on in any of the rooms?"

"Only in Falter's. I made a good mark, with the light coming from behind me."

"You were coming from Falter's room?"

Arnhardt hesitated for a perceptible period.

"Yes," he said gruffly. He got to his feet. "Rennert, I'm going to get this business settled tonight. Whoever shot me has still got the gun. If not he hasn't had a chance to throw it very far away. I'm going to search every room in this damned house. Want to go with me?" he demanded over his shoulder as he jerked open a drawer of the desk.

"Yes," Rennert replied, a worried frown on his forehead.

"O. K." Arnhardt turned about. In his right hand he held a blunt-nosed revolver. "Let's start."

"It might be well," Rennert suggested as he followed him out, "to look over the patio first. The gun may have been dropped. At any rate the shell should be on the ground."

"All right." Arnhardt was glancing over the enclosure, upon which light shone from three rooms—those of the Tolmans, Flores, and Miss Fahn.

Rennert stepped forward and ran the beam of the torch over the ground in front of the door. He considered footprints but realized that the hard baked surface would retain none. Arnhardt walked slowly at his side, his eyes on the wavering light.

"If it's in those damned flowers," he muttered, "we can let it go until daylight. It'd be like looking for a needle in a haystack." He stopped suddenly, with an exclamation, stooped over and picked up a bright object. He straightened up and held it out. Rennert centered the light upon it.

It was a spent cartridge.

"So this is where he stood." Arnhardt planted himself on the spot and his eyes swept the patio. They came to rest, Rennert noticed, on one lighted window. "Then it was easy enough to duck around the eaves to his door. Let's start on the rooms now." He dropped the cartridge into a pocket and moved forward.

Rennert followed him in silence. He was wishing that the young man wouldn't be quite so impulsive. He, had the feeling that nothing would come of this search yet had to admit that in his place he would probably have gone ahead as he was doing. The whole affair of the shooting bothered him. There was something about it that was at variance with the rest of the crimes that had been committed there. A direct and daring act whereas the poisonings had been carried out with a precision and a deliberateness of forethought that had so far safeguarded their perpetrator. Did this bullet sped into the darkness mean, he asked himself, that the latter was now striking out blindly in a panic of self-preservation?

Arnhardt had paused before the *sala*. Rennert stepped to his side and threw his light into it. It was deserted.

"If it's hidden in here we'll find it later," Arnhardt said. "In the meantime I'll lock the door." He turned the key in the lock and continued his way about the stone path.

They passed Rennert's doorway and stopped before Miss Fahn's.

"No use going in there," Arnhardt said after a moment's deliberation. "We might ask her, though, if she heard anything." He rapped on the door.

There was a scurrying sound from within and then dead silence. Arnhardt rapped again.

"Who's there?" came faintly from within.

"Arnhardt and Rennert, Miss Fahn. Can we come in?"

"Oh, no," it was a cry of consternation. Then: "Wait a minute."

They waited for perhaps two minutes, Arnhardt fidgeting in impatience. A key turned in the lock and there was the sound of a bolt being withdrawn. A thin crack of light emerged and in it the face of Miss Fahn.

"Oh, yes," she said with relief as she opened the door more widely. "I just wanted to be sure it was you."

She held a woolly kimono about her and was adjusting a lace cap over her hair. The ends of curlers protruded from the frills at its edges.

"What is it?" she was breathing heavily. "What has happened? What was that shot?"

Her eyes found Arnhardt's bandaged shoulder and she stepped back, the color receding from her face.

"Somebody shot me a few minutes ago," Arnhardt said bluntly. "We wondered if you'd heard anything."

Her face was gray lead. She said through tight lips: "Yes, I did. I did hear something. Somebody running outside."

"Running?" Rennert seized on this. "You heard this after or before the shot?"

"After. Right after. You see, I wasn't able to sleep after—after my experience with that Chinaman. I kept imagining I heard him coming back and fumbling at my door. So I was wide awake."

"Could you tell in what direction the footsteps went?"

"Out there," she gestured vaguely toward the window that faced the south and the mountains. "There was so much noise in the patio then that I couldn't be absolutely positive, though."

"Well, thanks, Miss Fahn," Arnhardt said. "You can go on to sleep now. We won't disturb you again."

She abandoned her last grip on the reins of control and was a terrified old woman.

"Sleep! I couldn't ever sleep in this place again. I want to get back home. I want daylight to come."

They left her staring straight ahead of her with fear-haunted eyes. The bolt slid quickly into place behind them.

"The old fool," Arnhardt said. "Always imagining she hears noises in the night. If she heard anything at all—and I doubt it—it was probably some coyote frightened by the shot." He passed the door of Falter's office, it was closed now, and paused at the arch-way. "He didn't go in there, I'm sure, or I would have seen him. Let's go ahead."

"Just a minute, Arnhardt." Rennert stopped him.

"I'd like to take a look in Lee's room while we're here."

"Lee? It couldn't have been him."

"No," Rennert said, "I don't think it was but it will do no harm to look."

As he spoke he flashed the light in the direction of the dining-room door. It stood open.

"This is usually locked, isn't it?" he asked as he walked toward it.

"Yes, Lee's supposed to lock it. With things in the state they've been tonight I don't suppose it's any wonder he forgot it."

Rennert went into the room, rounded the table and tried the handle of the door that opened onto the inner patio. It was un-locked.

They walked past the kitchen to the door of Lee's room. Rennert opened it softly and sent the yellow ray to the rumpled empty bed and about the bare gray walls.

Lee was not there.

23
ONE IS UNPERTURBED

ARNHARDT GAVE a sharp whistle of surprise. "That's strange. Lee usually goes to bed early." He looked at Rennert. "Say, I heard about him going in Miss Fahn's room tonight and frightening her with that knife. What was the matter with him? Drunk?"

"No," Rennert said slowly, "Lee wasn't drunk. He had been smoking *marihuana.*"

"*Marihuana!* Well, I'll be damned. I didn't know he used the stuff."

"I don't think he is in the habit of using it. This was left in his room in the form of cigarettes. He probably smoked them without knowing what was in them."

Arnhardt leaned against the door jamb, lightly balancing the revolver on the palm of his hand. He let his eyes stray to it then brought them back to Rennert's face.

"You mean someone left them there for him?"

"Yes."

"You don't suppose," with evident reluctance, "that it was Lee who shot me? That it was his steps Miss Fahn heard? They say that *marihuana* makes a man do insane things, things he wouldn't think of doing in his right mind."

This was exactly the possibility which Rennert was considering. He had his own explanation for the presence of the drugged cigarettes in Lee's room and felt sure that it was the correct one. The results, however, might be far different from those which the person who had put them there had anticipated. Witness the

132

attack on Miss Fahn, which he was sure had not been a part of this person's plan.

Arnhardt's laugh had a slight rasping sound.

"Oh, hell, I'm sure it wasn't Lee. Let's go look through the other rooms. I still think we'll find the gun in one of them."

They started toward the dining room. Rennert's torch strayed for an instant over the dark sea of flowers. He stopped.

"You go ahead," he said to Arnhardt, "I'll look through the rooms about this patio."

"That's right," the young man's eyes went from one door to the other. "Whoever shot me could have come through the dining room without passing under the archway, couldn't he?"

"Yes." Rennert's voice was abstracted. Evidently Arnhardt had not seen, as the light played over the patio, the figure that stood, still as one of the shadows about it, in the corner on the other side.

"Well, I'll go ahead," Arnhardt said. "Every minute gives more time to get that gun hidden."

Rennert repressed the observation that by now sufficient time had elapsed for any number of guns to be concealed. He waited until the other had gone, then walked across the patio. An effort at silence was useless on the crunching gravel of the walk. Halfway across he paused.

There was no sound at all yet he knew that someone was standing a few feet from him and, like himself, listening.

He had turned off the flashlight. Now he pressed its button.

The beam shot into the darkness and centered upon Maria Montemayor.

She stood under the eaves by a dense bed of yellow marigolds. In one hand she held a clay jug. At her feet rested a water bottle, its contents sparkling in the light. There was no alarm on her face, only a steady unblinking scrutiny after the first instant of adjustment of her eyes to the illumination.

"*Buenas noches*, Maria," Rennert said.

"*Buenas noches, señor*," they might have met in broad daylight, each on the most commonplace of errands.

"The flowers have thirst, do they not?" Rennert broke the silence.

"Yes, they have much thirst," her voice quickened into something like animation. "You understand?"

"I understand. They are so helpless, are they not? They ask so little. A little drop of water. They give beauty in return. They are generous."

"Yes, that is it," her smile was of delight in comprehension from this man with a white skin. "I hear them in the afternoon, when the sun is burning them. They call for something to drink. Just a little drop of water. When I can, I give it to them. They know me and thank me." Her voice sank into a soft murmur, "They have the voice of a little child."

"The one who is buried here?"

"Yes, señor, you know of him?"

"I have heard."

"And these," one hand fell and its fingers brushed lightly against the petals of a marigold that raised its head higher than the rest, "the *cempoalxochitl*, they served the Virgin today."

"By telling Miguel that he was to die?"

"Yes, she wanted to prepare him. She took away the white *claveles* that I put by his bed and put these in their place. They are the flowers of death, you know. But I did not understand. I would not see that the flowers were no longer white. Now I must not let these flowers die."

And thus, Rennert thought, *another miracle is born!* He kept his voice soft, conversational, using the half-toned diminutives and the gentle reverberation of ideas that mark the speech of the Mexican Indian. He was hoping that he could preserve this mood of mutual confidence until he had acquired the information which he was sure this woman held.

"Did the flowers have a message of death for your son as well as Miguel?" he asked.

"No," she shook her head and vagueness smoothed her face, "they had no message for him. It was because of the doctor, the *medico* from the city."

"They brought a doctor from the city then?"

"Yes, Señor Stahl thought that a doctor could help him. He did not know. My son died. That is why, señor, I did not wish a doctor for Miguel."

"The doctor gave him medicine?"

"Yes, he left the medicine."

"The boy took all of it?"

"No. After the doctor left he took no more. But it was too late then to save him."

"And this medicine—you kept it?"

"No, señor."

"What became of it?"

"I do not know, señor. The doctor left it there," she gestured toward Falter's office, "for them to give to the boy."

Rennert felt a pleasurable surge of excitement. Again he was on the path, straight and well defined as the graveled one on which he stood, that he had left earlier for a brief and futile excursion. He came back to what was for him now a triviality.

"You have watered the flowers each night?" he asked.

"Yes, señor, each night."

"And your key to the kitchen where the water is kept?"

"Here," in disarming childlike confidence Maria pulled from the folds of her dress a string at the end of which dangled a key. "I did not lose it, no. I told them—the others—that I had lost it. They would not understand and would not have permitted me to use the water."

"And Lee, the *chino?*"

"Ah, that one!" there was a flicker of contempt in her voice. "He is sleeping."

"You have been here in the patio how long?"

"A few little moments, señor."

Rennert knew the difficulty of extracting measurements of time in this land where time is meaningless.

He asked: "You were here before the shot in the other patio?"

"Yes, much before." The matter of the shot remained an event of no interest to her except to fix time upon.

"And Lee did not pass through this patio?"

"No, señor, he did not pass. I would have heard him."

"There are places near by where one could hide, are there not?"

"In the mountains there are many places."

Rennert stepped past her, flashed the light into the bathroom. It was, as he had thought it would be, empty.

"The rains will come tonight, I think, Maria," he said as he returned. "There will be plenty of water. But these last few weeks men have needed this water. Did you not think of them?"

"Yes, señor, but I myself have drunk little water so that the flowers could have more. They could do the same. The flowers," she said softly, "were here before men."

She stood, the embodiment of the Mexico that stands self-sufficient by the side of the road while conquering armies march by, to be replaced in days or years or centuries (it doesn't matter) by other armies under other banners. *Along the paved highway to the east,* Rennert thought, *will come another, more dreadful army with billboards and refreshment stands and blatant automobile horns, but Maria and her kind will stand when they have passed by.*

"*Buenas noches,*" he said quietly.

"*Buenas noches, señor.*"

As he walked away he heard behind him the gentle splash of water.

He stood in the door of Flores' room and watched Arnhardt push shut a steamer trunk. Beside him were an alligator-skin grip and the black leather case which Rennert had seen in the Mexican's hands the afternoon before. He flung the grip on the bed and began to rummage through its contents with his free hand.

Flores stood to one side, placidly smoking a cigarette. He looked up at Rennert.

"Come in, Mr. Rennert, and join in the search," his pleasantly modulated voice held an undercurrent of raillery. "I suppose you know that Mr. Arnhardt is searching for a gun. Really you should have him on duty at the border to examine the luggage of the tourists and the school teachers from Kansas who come down to see our picturesque country. He is most thorough." As he spoke his eyes went to Arnhardt's back and there was a slight widening of his fixed smile.

After a moment's contemplation of the scene Rennert walked slowly and as if at random to the leather case, noticing obliquely the expression on the Mexican's face. He saw, for the merest fraction of time, a calculating look come into the dark eyes. It was gone then and Flores moved a step in his direction, saying: "Mr. Arnhardt has already examined that, Mr. Rennert. It is a little invention of mine." He paused and pronounced the words with distinct emphasis, "A radio attachment."

Arnhardt closed the grip with a snap and set it on the floor.

"Yes," he said to Rennert, "I looked through that case. Nothing but a bunch of metal and wires. Let's go. Sorry to have bothered you, Flores, but we've got to search all the rooms, you know."

That, Rennert thought, *is exactly what you are not doing*. There was a precipitousness about Arnhardt's movements, an eagerness to get ahead with this perfunctory search that puzzled him. He thought: *He acts as if he knew beforehand what the result will be.*

"I am very glad that you have found nothing, Mr. Arnhardt." Flores' voice was too suave, faintly metallic. "If you had found a gun it would have been very hard for me to explain, would it not?"

"Damn right it would!" Arnhardt's mouth was twisted in a grin.

"You have, however, neglected to look in one place."

Arnhardt frowned at him.

"Where's that?"

"On my person." Flores held his arms slightly away from his body, inviting search.

"Oh," Arnhardt hesitated. "That's right. I didn't suppose you'd be fool enough to keep it on you, if you had it." He ran his hand quickly over Flores' body.

"Nor would I be such a fool," the Mexican said evenly. "That is all, Mr. Arnhardt?"

"That's all, yes."

"Good night, then. We have here in Mexico the saying 'My house is yours.' It is literally true in this case."

"Good night."

Outside, Arnhardt's steps quickened as he moved toward Tolman's room.

"The last place," he said grimly. "We might as well have begun on this side of the patio and saved ourselves some trouble."

"You expect to find the gun here then?" Rennert had to ask.

Arnhardt stopped and stared for a moment straight ahead of him.

"Rennert," he said stiffly, "I told you that I had suspected somebody all along of poisoning my stepfather. Well, it was Tolman. I wanted to be fair, though, and look in the other rooms first. Just on the chance that I might be wrong." His fist began to beat a tattoo on the wood.

"Hello, Tolman," he said as the door was opened. "We're looking for the gun that somebody used tonight. Your room's next on the list."

Tolman stood motionless, one hand about the knob. The light, striking his face sideways, brought out the bloodlessness of his skin and the dark hollows of his eyes.

"I suppose," he said in a low voice, "that my assurance that I didn't shoot you would not be sufficient?"

"No, it won't. I'm sorry but everybody would say the same thing, of course."

Tolman's eyes went to Rennert's face then slowly back to Arnhardt.

"Very well," he stepped aside, "come in."

Arnhardt pushed past him and began the search. He worked, Rennert noticed, more methodically this time, concentrating his attention on each article of furniture in turn. Tolman stood before the door, his eyes following the other's movements. One corner of his lower lip was drawn in and wedged tightly between his teeth.

Arnhardt finally finished with the dresser and the table and was passing the window to the clothes closet when he came to an abrupt stop, his eyes on the window. With a swift movement he stepped to it, stooped over and caught hold of something at the base of the vertical bar. He moved back, pulling.

It was a string that passed over the ledge to hang outside. Rennert's ears caught the scraping on the adobe and knew before Arnhardt gave a final triumphant jerk that a pistol was attached to the end.

24
ONE IS PERTURBED

IT WAS A COLT AUTOMATIC. The caliber was forty-five. The pistol which Rennert had seen in the drawer of Falter's desk was a forty-five Colt automatic.

Arnhardt jerked loose the string which had been tied about its butt and held it in his outstretched hand. His eyes rested accusingly on Tolman's face.

"Well?" his voice flicked.

Tolman stood in the same lifeless posture. His shoulders had drooped a little and his face had gone even whiter than before. His eyes did not waver from their fixed stare at the gun.

"I'm sorry, Tolman," Arnhardt's voice carried no sympathy; "I was afraid it was you all the time. I kept still when my stepfather was poisoned. When the same thing happened to Miguel and Falter it was too much. Now its self-defence with me. I say I'm sorry for Ann's sake."

Tolman winced. He raised his eyes very slowly and looked at Arnhardt and then at Rennert. There was a haggard, trapped look in them.

"You think I killed those men?" he asked in a low dogged tone.

Arnhardt shrugged.

"I don't see how you can deny it now."

"I didn't, though." Tolman spoke in the same voice. "I got that gun from Falter's desk, yes. But I didn't shoot you."

Arnhardt's laugh was ugly.

"A likely story. What did you get it for then?" The other hesitated and his eyes wandered away to the window.

"For protection," he said through set lips.

Arnhardt laughed again in open derision.

"Expect us to believe that?"

Rennert had been following the scene with close though unobtrusive attention.

"We might," he said to Arnhardt now, "examine the magazine and be sure that a shot has been fired."

Arnhardt fumbled with the gun then handed it to Rennert.

"You look. I can't manage it with one hand."

Rennert drew out the magazine and extracted the round from the chamber. It was half full. He squinted down the barrel, then looked at Arnhardt.

"Are you an expert on ballistics?"

"No."

Rennert put the gun together again.

"Neither am I. There's no telling then whether or not this has been fired recently. I suppose you noticed, however, that the barrel does not seem to be warm."

Arnhardt put out his hand for it.

"That probably doesn't mean anything. It's had time to cool off, hanging out there in the air." He thrust it into a hip pocket. "In the morning," he said to Tolman, "I'm going in to Victoria for the authorities. I'd advise you to be here when I get back."

Tolman maintained his silence.

Arnhardt turned to the door.

"And remember there's nothing but desert and mountains around this place. It's a hell of a long ways to a railroad." He turned and tramped heavily out of the room.

There was a long strained silence in his wake. Tolman's breath began to come and go audibly. He moved toward the bed, as if blindly, and sank down on it. He held his hands loosely folded and stared at the window.

"Arnhardt didn't shoot himself, you know," Rennert said quietly. "There were no powder burns on his clothing."

Tolman looked up slowly, as if just aware of his presence.

"There weren't?" he said blankly. "No, I suppose not."

"I think," Rennert said, "that you had better confide in me."

"About what?"

"Why you took that gun. Why you hung it out the window, so that it couldn't be seen in this room. You must realize as well as I the situation you're in."

Tolman looked away.

"I haven't anything to say, Mr. Rennert."

Rennert regarded him for a moment, recognized the indomitability in the voice and in the indrawn look on the stiff white face.

"If you change your mind," he said quietly, "come and talk to me at once."

"All right." Tolman's thin lips scarcely moved. Rennert left him, walked across the patio and tapped lightly on Falter's door.

Ann Tolman opened it.

"Come in, Mr. Rennert." She closed the door and faced him. Her eyes were red and deep lines about the corners of her lips showed how tightly she was holding them in control. "Mr. Falter is dead," she said tonelessly. "He died a few minutes ago."

Rennert went into the other room and approached the bed. He looked down at the still face, its skin under the blotching tan as white as the coverings. His fingers found the pulse and released it. He took out his watch and held the crystal close to the half open mouth. He pulled a sheet slowly over the body and left it.

Ann Tolman was standing in the other room. She had not moved. She looked at him and said tonelessly: "There's no doubt, I suppose?"

"No, there is no doubt."

She half-closed her eyes and let her head sink. "It's so terrible," she said, "to think that we knew he was dying—and couldn't do anything."

"Now, Mrs. Tolman, there is something else you must do."

"What is it?" She raised her head listlessly.

"You knew that Mark Arnhardt and I have been looking for the gun with which he was shot?"

"Yes, I supposed that is what you were doing. I went to your room but you weren't there."

"We found a gun in your husband's room, Mrs. Tolman. Did you know it was there?"

Her eyes widened and she put out a hand to grasp his sleeve.

"A gun?" her voice was stripped of everything save sheer fright.

"Yes, a Colt automatic."

"No, no!" she shook her head wildly. "There must be some mistake. Steve doesn't have a gun."

Rennert said evenly as his eyes searched her face: "He took that gun from the drawer of the desk here. This evening."

"But—" She faltered. Then, swiftly, "Did he say that?"

"Yes."

Her face might have been of frozen dead flesh.

"I think that you had better go to him, Mrs. Tolman. He had a purpose in taking it. I suppose you realize that?"

She nodded numbly.

"Go now, Mrs. Tolman. I'll stay here for the rest of the night."

He opened the door for her and she went out, walking with the steps of an automaton.

Rennert stood for several minutes under the eaves, smoking. Then he walked to Arnhardt's door and knocked.

It was unlocked and thrown open and Arnhardt faced him. He had removed his shirt and his muscular arms and shoulders were dark bronze in the light that came from behind them.

"Oh, hello, Rennert," he said flatly. He raised his chin. "If you don't mind I'd rather not talk about it any more tonight. My mind's made up and I want to get some sleep."

"I wasn't intending to talk about Tolman. I wanted to tell you first that Falter has just died."

"Oh," Arnhardt stared past him. "I suppose," he said inflectionlessly, "that you weren't surprised?"

"There's nothing to be done tonight, is there?"

"Nothing. There is, however, a question I want to ask you."

"Yes?"

"It's about Miguel and Maria Montemayor's son. Were you here when he died several weeks ago?"

"Yes," surprise was in the voice.

"There was a doctor in attendance on him, I understand."

"Yes, a doctor from Victoria. Maria didn't want him but when the boy kept getting worse Stahl insisted on getting him. I don't think she ever forgave him for doing it. She had been dosing him with herbs. Probably caused his death herself."

"It was helminthiasis—worms—wasn't it?"

"Yes."

"Do you know what medicine the doctor gave him?"

"No, I haven't any idea. I remember that he left some, though, with directions for us to see that Maria gave it to the boy."

"Do you know what became of that medicine?"

"No, I don't. I suppose it was thrown out."

"That's all, then, Arnhardt. Thank you."

As he crossed the patio he glanced from room to room. All were dark save Falter's office, Arnhardt's, and Tolman's. Before he walked on, however, his eyes had detected a thin pencil of light that came from Flores' window, where a cloth had been fastened over the bars.

Esteban Flores was sitting upon the edge of a chair, very still, and staring at the door through which Rennert and Arnhardt had gone. At his feet stood the alligator-skin grip and the black leather case. Half-opened drawers in the dresser still bore testimony to the futile search that had destroyed the tidiness of the room. The air was stale, faintly pungent with the odors of the flowers that crept in through the blankets that covered the window, and mephitic with the clouds of tobacco smoke that hung motionless between him and the ceiling.

Fear verging on panic ran through him coldly, giving an iciness to the trickles of perspiration that made their way from the border of his pomade-sleek hair down the side of his head and under the collar of his green silk pajamas. He wanted desperately to leave that lonely hacienda that was for him again a place of vague, uneasy misgivings. As it had been in the days of his childhood, when he had sat very still, just as he was sitting now, and had listened to relatives, pompous and unapproachable in brocade and unbendable starchiness, talk of their elders who had died there and relate with arrogant smiling lips tales of the *tecolote* that the peons claimed to have heard wailing in flight over the roof. Their eyes, he remembered, had never smiled.

He thought with sudden terrible loneliness of Madero Avenue in the capital, with its electric beer signs and honking taxis, of Prendes', filled with alcoholic after-the-theater chatter. The aroma of some flower in the patio was insistent, as it was every night, with memories of the musky perfume that clung to soft pink silk in a certain bedroom off the street of Isabel the Catholic.

His eyes pierced the visions and came to rest on the black leather case. For the first time skepticism edged itself into his mind. Perhaps, after all, this instrument acquired with such secrecy in that Mexico City shop and invested with such anticipatory dreams was—as he had heard it hinted—a fraud, believed in only by fools.

An idea brought him to his feet, his breath coming and going more rapidly. He stared at the thermometer which hung on the wall beside the door. There had been all the time the possibility of proof—definite proof easily obtained.

He unlocked the case and took out the instrument with careful eager fingers. He felt the need of haste now. Anything to end the uncertainty that was tormenting him.

He set up in the middle of the floor the tripod that supported three metal bars in the shape of an equilateral triangle. He straightened the two gossamer-thin wires that hung from the top bar and came together to form the vertex of another smaller triangle. He touched with his index finger the slender piece of wood, stripped of bark, which was suspended from this second triangle like the base of a Y.

He took down the thermometer and regarded the mercury speculatively. It stood, he noticed, at 92 degrees. Strange that it should have risen in such a short time while the air in the room had grown steadily hotter and closer. Then he remembered the blankets at the windows. They, of course, accounted for it.

He came back and waited until the wood had stopped swaying, was entirely motionless. Then he got down on his knees and laid the thermometer flat on the floor, a foot or so away. His eyes stayed on the wood as if attracted by a magnet.

He moved the thermometer nearer, a few inches at a time. At last he picked it up with tight fingers and laid it directly under the tip of the wood.

His eyes remained fixed for sixty full seconds, ticked off mockingly by his wrist-watch.

He got up then and a great weariness went over him. It wasn't from any exertion of that day but the cumulative effects of weeks of suspense, buoyed up by a hope that now had crumbled to fragments. The scent of musk and silk-soft flesh faded. His mouth felt bitter.

25
VALKYRIES RIDE NORTH

THE WIND AWOKE RENNERT. It came through the open window, not in intermittent gusts, but as a steady relentless current propelled by the blades of a gigantic electric fan whose dynamo emitted the droning crescendo hum that was its accompaniment. Once inside it abandoned pretense of innocence and swirled madly in eddies that ripped across the floor, raising the dust in tiny staggering columns to break against the walls and reform in other smaller spouts moving ever toward the window again.

He got up from the chair where he had succumbed at last to fitful uneasy sleep, broken by vague stirrings of alarm at unaccustomed sounds that had been, he knew now, the scouts of the wind, testing the adobe walls with exploratory fingers. He stretched wearily and went to the window.

There was no sun. They were imprisoned beneath a lid of watery-gray lead, solidly convex, obscured by scudding fragmentary clouds of lighter dirty gray that tore themselves like steam from the boiling mass that bulged the southwestern horizon.

The yucca tree at the corner was stripped of its blossoms and its sharp leaves were bent toward the northeast. On the stone bench under the tree a figure was huddled as if dropped there inanimate by the wind.

Rennert stared at it for a moment then went outside. The patio was filled with swirling petals and leaves that mingled in rainbow hues to be separated and drawn together again by irresistible suction and sent upwards over the walls. The branches of the frangipani tree were whipping the eaves and its white flowers were sailing, like lost parachutes, in the crosscurrents.

He made his way out the door and had to brace himself as he walked into the face of the wind. He stood and looked down at the man asleep on the bench. It was Lee. His mouth was half open and he was breathing in long gasps.

Rennert leaned over and prodded him. Lee wriggled and turned his head. Rennert shook him. Lee opened his eyes and looked at him dazedly.

"What's matter, boss?" he asked thickly.

"Get up," Rennert told him.

Lee sat up and rubbed his fists across his bloodshot eyes. He gazed about him.

"What the hell? I been sleep out here?"

"I should judge, Lee, that you slept here all night." Lee shook his head.

"No lemember, boss, no lemember. Head hurt like hell. Jaw hurt like hell," he ran a doubtful finger down it. "Think I'm sick."

"No, you aren't sick," Rennert took him by an arm and got him to his feet. "Move around and you'll be all right. You might fix some breakfast now."

Lee started toward the door, mouthing a jumble of sounds that were lost in the wind. Rennert accompanied him in silence through the patio and into the kitchen. He took a cigarette from his pocket and held it on his palm.

"I found some of these on a chair in your room last night," he said. "They are yours?"

Lee came nearer and peered down. He shook his head emphatically.

"Not mine. Somebody leave 'em in my room. I smoke some last night. Get sick like hell. Head go like this," he waved a hand furiously around and around.

Rennert returned the cigarette to his pocket. "First time you ever smoked *marihuana*, Lee?"

Lee paused with his hand still in the air.

"That *marihuana?*" he demanded

"Yes."

"You keep 'em and smoke 'em, Mistah Rennert. You get sick too. Sick like hell."

"Tell me what you remember after you smoked the cigarettes, Lee."

"All gone, all gone," he tapped his forehead lightly. "No lemember much. Think I tell Miss Fahn go to hell."

"You mean you told her last night?"

"Yes, think so. Tell her too damn hot to wear goddamn jacket." He shook his head. "All dark then. Don't lemember nothing. Out in dark. Go to sleep on bench. Miss Fahn run out looking for me. I too sleepy to tell her to go to hell Go back to sleep. You wake me up."

"You say that Miss Fahn came out of the house?" Rennert was alert.

"Think so. Looking for me. Mad like hell. Always mad like hell."

"Could you see her in the dark?"

"Not see her, no. Hear her running. Big feet made lots noise on glavel."

"But you're not sure, then, that it was Miss Fahn?"

"Think so, boss. She looking for me, want to fire me. I tell her go to hell. Give me cigarette, please. Not *marihuana*, good United States cigarette. I be all light now."

Rennert gave him the cigarette and left him. His face had a preoccupied frown as he walked into the patio again and made his way to the bathroom

He was familiar enough with the effects of *marihuana* to know how little credence one could put in the distorted images that played before the senses of the person under its influence. He knew too that these images, once they were brought into proper focus, might be revelatory of actual occurrences. Lee's animosity toward Miss Fahn, for example, was real enough, coloring his emotions to an extraordinary degree. As he considered the inferences to be drawn from the wisps of memory in the Chinaman's brain he felt his excitement mounting. He experienced an odd exhilaration as if a weight that had pressed down upon his head and the nape of his neck for hours had been removed. There was a tingling in his body like that which ran through his fingers when he passed them across his hair. As the atmosphere was being swept clean of stagnancy so was his mind racing swiftly toward a solution of the case

As he ran the razor over the stubble on his face he was viewing again the puzzle-picture which he had completed during the long hours of the night, when he had sat in an uncomfortable chair in the anteroom of death. When the design had first taken shape before his steep-ridden eyes the sheer audacity which it represented had kept him at first from accepting it. Now in the gray light of morning he realized how utterly simple it had been from the first, once the relevant was separated from the irrelevant. He faced the bitter and inescapable fact that the agent of one of the murders which had taken place on the hacienda was innocent. He winced as the blade nicked his skin. Fatuously innocent, he told himself grimly.

Mentally he scrambled the pieces and began to put them together again: the poisoned candy, whisky, and tablets which in quick succession had stricken Stahl, Miguel, and Falter; that other death which had put the instrument of killing into a potential murderer's hand; the glass-domed upper floor of the building which existed as yet only on Stephen Tolman's drawing-board. Each slipped neatly into its groove, leaving a surface so smoothly welded that it satisfied perfectly his passion for exactitude.

And next? He rubbed his face hard with the towel. He didn't know what to do next. Except wait. . . .

As he left the room he met Esteban Flores making his way in that direction. In his hand he held a shaving-kit and a towel. He looked sleepy, tousled by the wind and stripped of the veneer of sleekness that had covered him.

"Good morning, Mr. Rennert."

"Good morning." Rennert had not realized before how young the fellow was.

When he had disappeared into the bathroom Rennert crossed quickly to the room which he had vacated. He stood looking about him speculatively.

The evidences of intended departure were apparent. The trunk was locked and evidently packed with the clothing which had hung in the now empty wardrobe. The grip lay open on the bed, half-filled with shirts and underwear. Between them was the black leather case.

Rennert knelt beside this, took a thin steel instrument from his pocket and inserted it in the lock. A deft turn of the wrist and it flew open.

He spent perhaps two minutes examining it then emitted a low whistle, half of surprise, half of satisfaction, and put the instrument back in its case. He locked this and left the room. Flores, he knew now, had caught a glimpse of the will-o'-the-wisp that dances eternally over the mountains of Mexico, tempting the sanest onto the trail of blood and disillusionment Young, indeed, and gullible. . . .

Mark Arnhardt was standing by the fountain, gazing up at the sky. There was a solid statuesque effect of strength unconscious of itself about his body, outlined in all its impressive muscularity by the wind that tore at his clothing. He pushed hair back from his forehead and looked at Rennert with eyes that showed no early-morning sleepiness.

"Looks as if we were in for a blow," he commented.

"Yes, the force of the wind is increasing steadily."

They remained without speaking for a moment, watching the torn fragments of clouds that raced toward the hacienda as if intent on its destruction. *Valkyries*, Rennert thought, *choosing a spot to dip their lances again!*

"Been up long?" Arnhardt asked.

"About an hour. How's the arm?" Rennert eyed the bandage.

"All right. By the way, I forgot to ask you last night if you had examined those fingerprints?"

"I wondered," Rennert smiled slightly, "if you were going to disregard those prints entirely."

Arnhardt's eyes were hard and cold as they surveyed the sky. The wind robbed his voice of any inflection it may have had. "It's not hard to guess whose prints you found on that caramel."

Rennert said: "You're wrong, Mr. Arnhardt. I examined them very carefully last night. It is very hard indeed to guess whose prints I found there."

It seemed to take a moment for the significance of Rennert's words to penetrate to Arnhardt's mind. He was breathing deeply and regularly as if exulting silently in the wild pageantry of the skies. His eyes came slowly to Rennert's face. There was a steel-hard stare in them.

"You mean," he said, "that they weren't Tolman's?"

"Exactly, Mr. Arnhardt, they were not Tolman's."

26
THE PRESENCE OF MURDER

Very deliberately Arnhardt reached down and pulled loose a leaf from a scarlet runner that had crept over the lip of the fountain. He took the tip between his teeth, bit it in two and spat out the fragment.

"Whose prints were they then?" He spoke to the wind.

"I can't say at present, Mr. Arnhardt."

"What do you mean—you can't say?"

"Just that."

Arnhardt centered his attention on the leaf.

"Were they George Stahl's?"

"No, they were not Stahl's."

"See here, Rennert," Arnhardt crushed the leaf between his fingers and flung it from him, "you're being mighty secretive about this."

"Sorry," Rennert shrugged, "I'm not being so purposely. I simply mean what I say. I cannot tell you at present whose prints they are."

Arnhardt regarded him steadily.

"I see now," he said slowly, "why you acted the way you did last night when I accused Tolman of shooting me. You knew his prints weren't on that caramel."

"Exactly."

"Well," he heaved himself from his perch, "regardless of those prints we've got a case against Tolman now. That gun."

"It seems to me, Arnhardt, that you have no case at all against him."

"The hell I haven't!"

"You know that the person who shot you used an automatic. That's all. It will be necessary to find the bullet and to prove that it was fired from the gun which Tolman had in his room. That will require the services of an expert."

"All right, I'll get an expert then. I've stood this delay as long as I'm going to. I'm getting the authorities in from Victoria this morning, just like I said I would. Now, what about some breakfast?"

"What I was going to suggest."

"Wonder if Lee's up?"

"Yes, the meal should be ready by now."

The first pellets of rain struck their faces, hard as buckshot. There was a drumming on the tiles.

The dining room was bleak and cheerless in the gray half-light, filled with flying particles of dust, and the adobe walls exuded a dank chill.

Arnhardt switched on the electric light and grimaced as he looked about him.

"Did you ever see a Mexican dining room that didn't take away your appetite?" he asked as he sat down.

"Especially at breakfast time," Rennert agreed. "And it's a bad enough meal in any place."

"The Mexicans don't seem to mind it." Arnhardt tapped the bell.

"No, their conversational pyrotechnics at breakfast always amaze me."

Arnhardt's eyes rested for an unguarded instant on the empty chair at the head of the table and a frown darkened his face. He took them away quickly and stared straight down at the tablecloth in complete tight-lipped absorption.

The screaming of the wind outside accented the long silence that stood between them.

Arnhardt roused himself at last, with visible effort, and tapped at the bell again.

Lee came in from the kitchen. With an unsteady hand he reached over to the center of the table for the glass jug of coffee, poured a little into the two cups and filled them brim full with luke-warm milk.

"What in the hell were you so long about?" Arnhardt demanded irritably.

"Don't feel good this morning, boss. Head hurt like hell. Not work much today. Get some sleep. Eggs same way?"

Arnhardt said with heavy sarcasm: "Yes, I'll have eggs for a change. The same way." He frowned at the man's back and said to Rennert: "Always eggs down here! And to think I used to order 'em out of choice! I'd give a ten-dollar bill right now for a few strips of crisp bacon and a cup of real honest-to-god coffee." He eyed distastefully the pile of mangoes halfway between them. "Lee looks as if he'd had a bad night. Did you find out where he was when we went to his room?"

"He spent the night on the bench under the yucca tree."

"He did?" Arnhardt frowned, started to say something and changed his mind as Flores entered.

He was freshly shaven and his hair glistened like black patent leather. With pomade, face lotion and, unmistakably, perfume he had slipped on again his air of assurance. He stood with one hand on the back of his chair and bowed slightly in Arnhardt's direction.

"Good morning, Mr. Arnhardt."

Arnhardt made an indeterminate sound with his tongue.

"How are you this morning, Mr. Rennert?" Another bow. He sat down and unfolded his napkin with a distinct flourish. He began delicately to finger the mangoes. Presently he found one to his satisfaction, removed it to his plate and, plunging a two-pronged fork into the end, began deftly to peel it.

"How," he asked without looking up, "is Mr. Falter this morning?"

Rennert watched Lee emerging from the kitchen.

"He died this morning."

Flores deposited a strip of peeling upon his plate and regarded it thoughtfully.

"What a pity!" His eyes slowly detached themselves from the peeling and went to Rennert's face, searched for something that they did not find.

Lee placed fried eggs before Rennert and Arnhardt.

"*Blanquillos, Señor Flores?*" he asked dully.

"*Sí.*" Flores looked down at the mango speculatively, found a starting point and buried his teeth in the rich ripe fruit. He finished one side, laid the fork and its burden down and touched his lips with his napkin. "You do not like the mango, Mr. Rennert?"

"Yes, ordinarily I like it very much. This morning its sweet taste doesn't appeal to me. Coffee is my main craving."

"You are upset. Yes, that is it. When one's stomach is not in order the mango does not appeal so much." He began to slice the remainder into long yellow strips. "'This is the *mango de Manila.* I much prefer the smaller variety. They are richer and sweeter, with a green tinge to their flesh. On the other hand the kernel is very large. There should be a cross between the two. Are you acquainted with our tropical fruits, Mr. Rennert? They offer an endless variety for breakfast. One could in the city have a different kind each morning for a month. Bananas alone, for instance. There is the big 'male banana' and the very sweet little bananas. Besides the bananas with yellow flesh, the kind you are accustomed to in the United States, there are those with pink, orange . . ."

He talked on to the accompaniment of the rising drone of the wind. Dust was everywhere—irritation in the eyes, grit against the teeth, a thin film of grayness on the tablecloth. The rain beat on the tiles might have been on their skulls.

Rennert saw Arnhardt glance up at the door and quickly lower his gaze.

Ann and Stephen Tolman came in. Her "good morning" collided with that of Rennert and of Flores with a cheerfulness that did nothing but heighten the tension of the room. Arnhardt said nothing but broke a roll with such emphasis that the fragments of crust flew over the cloth. Stephen Tolman looked at none of them but made his way to his chair in a lost fashion. Ann took a cup and saucer from the table and went into the kitchen.

Flores made an attempt to sweep Tolman into the orbit of tropical fruits: "What is it that you call the *aguacate* in the United States, Mr. Tolman? Avocados sometimes but there is another name."

Tolman shook his head without replying.

"Alligator pears," Rennert contributed.

"Yes, that is it. I could never understand why such a name was given to them. Perhaps a misunderstanding of the pronunciation. Is it a fruit or a vegetable? A vegetable, I believe you consider it, although it grows on a tree . . ."

Talking, Rennert thought, *in a desperate attempt to keep from looking at that empty chair and thinking about the ugliness of murder.* He watched Ann emerge from the kitchen, approach the table and pour coffee into the cup that she had half-filled with milk.

"I'm taking this to Miss Fahn," she explained to no one in particular. "She isn't feeling well this morning."

Something about the way she said it, an odd nervous lightness, made Rennert glance at her sharply. As she put the cup and saucer upon a plate and laid a roll beside it her eyes met his for an instant. There was a clouded troubled look in them that he knew came from some deeper cause than sleeplessness.

He got up and followed her into the patio. She stood waiting for him, braced against the wall and staring straight at the fountain.

He came closer to her and said as low as he could in the screaming of the wind: "What's the matter, Mrs. Tolman?"

"It's Miss Fahn." The wind caught the words and whipped them away.

"She isn't seriously ill, is she?"

The cup rattled against the plate. Rennert glanced at the swirling coffee and took it from her trembling hands.

"I don't know," she said. "I think it's mostly fright. She came to my room this morning and asked me if I would bring her this coffee." She hesitated, and Rennert had to lean forward to understand her. "She was afraid to eat anything and I had to assure her that I would pour the coffee and the milk myself. After everyone else had, taken some first. It's poison she's afraid of."

"Lee?"

"Yes, I think so. I really can't blame her after last night."

"Tell her that there's nothing to worry about on that score. She can drink that coffee and eat that roll without danger. I'll explain to her later." He studied her face. "You have something else on your mind."

"Yes," her voice shook uncontrollably. "I'm not sure about Miss Fahn. That it is all fright. She has a headache. Her ears hurt, she says."

"She still feels the pressure on them?"

"Yes." She raised her hands and pressed the palms against her own ears. "And I feel it too—something's wrong with them!"

"It's only the effects of the storm," he said. "There's nothing to worry about."

Her eyes were on his face.

"You feel it yourself then?"

He smiled reassuringly.

"Yes, Mrs. Tolman, we all feel it."

"And you're sure it's nothing but the storm?"

"Positive."

She put out a hand.

"I can carry the plate then. You see, I was afraid it was—something else." As she spoke her eyes went swiftly through the oblique swaying curtain of rain to the closed door of Falter's room.

27
CHALLENGE

IN THE DINING ROOM conversation was at a standstill. Arnhardt's eggs, half-eaten, lay congealing on his plate. He had lit a cigarette and was staring down at them with a preoccupied air. Tolman was still eating his mango, half-heartedly, as his inexpert fingers tried to keep the fork fastened in the flesh. He seemed listless, drained of vitality, and there were dark violet pouches under his eyes. Flores, with a fragment of bread, was dexterously removing a last rivulet of yellow yolk from his plate.

As Rennert came in and sat down he saw Tolman's eyes seek his. He answered the unspoken question: "There's nothing wrong with Miss Fahn. It is merely the disturbance in the atmosphere that is causing her headache and the feeling in her ears."

Tolman's gaze rested for several seconds on Rennert's face as if trying to force by its directness a further admission. He seemed satisfied at last and said very distinctly: "I was sure it was nothing serious but Ann was a bit worried."

Arnhardt rubbed out the stub of his cigarette and lit another.

Rennert thought: *When a habitual pipe smoker takes to cigarettes he is on a decided nervous strain.* He drained his coffee cup and said to Arnhardt: "I wonder if you'd mind ringing for Lee? I think I could do with another cup of coffee."

Arnhardt raised his hand and let it fall on the bell. The sharp peal seemed to send vibrations humming through the tautened air of the room.

Lee padded across the tiles to Arnhardt's elbow. His eyes were blinking as if lighting off sleep. "Yes, boss?"

"Bring Mr. Rennert a cup of hot milk, Lee. He wants another cup of coffee."

"I believe," Rennert said, "that I'll take hot water this time. A very little bit." It was, he knew, an admission of his own uneasiness before this dead weight of uncertainty that hung over them. Waiting and drinking black coffee until the murderer should make another move.

Lee nodded and went out.

Tolman got up and ran a hand along the edge of the tablecloth. On the side facing the door it was moving in little ripples as the deflected wind struck it.

"I don't suppose," he said, "that this storm is likely to be serious? That there's any real danger?"

"Not much danger, I should think," Rennert said. "The mountains between here and the coast have broken the force of it, undoubtedly. What we are getting is merely the last of it."

"I'm glad to hear you say that. I didn't want Ann to worry." He turned and walked away.

Flores watched him go and then said calmly as he smoothed out the sides of a cigarette: "What we *will* get, Mr. Rennert. The full force of the hurricane is just now reaching us. The rain will continue to fall for some time. Then it will slacken. The wind will stop and we will think it is over. That will be but a lull. How long it will last there is no knowing. As soon as it has passed," he slipped the cigarette between his lips and raised his voice slightly, "I am leaving."

There was silence that seemed prolonged unbearably. If it could be called silence in this vacuum-like place hemmed in by the sucking eddies of the wind

Arnhardt sat up very straight in his chair. His face was stony.

"What was that you said, Flores?"

"I think you heard me, Mr. Arnhardt," the Mexican began to play with a folder of wax matches. "I am leaving for Mexico City as soon as possible. This afternoon at the latest."

"How, may I ask?"

Flores struck a match and applied it to the end of the cigarette. "In my plane."

"It's not damaged then?" There was an ominous quietness in Arnhardt's voice.

"No, it is not damaged." Flores' fingers laid the match carefully upon the side of his plate. A thin trickle of smoke came from his nostrils.

"You've been lying about it all the time then?"

A shrug and a deprecating gesture with the hands.

"Let us call it exaggerating, Mr. Arnhardt. There is always some slight disarrangement of the parts of a plane."

Arnhardt sent his cigarette spinning in the direction of the doorway, where the wind caught it and sent it to the floor.

"No one," he said, "is leaving this place until I say so."

The expression of Flores' face did not change beyond a slight contraction of the pupils of his eyes. As he spoke his lips drew apart so that his teeth gleamed. "You speak very confidently, Mr. Arnhardt. May I ask what is going to prevent me from leaving when I wish?"

Arnhardt's right hand went to his hip. It came out holding the blunt-nosed revolver.

"This," he laid it on the table with a thud.

Flores' black eyebrows rose in thin arcs. He sent two streams of smoke through his nostrils. They came slowly, two parallel streams, with a steady force that seemed unending. At last they ceased and he said: "The gun for which you were looking last night?"

"No, but it will serve."

"You found the other gun then?"

"Yes."

"Since it was not found among my effects what, may I ask, am I accused of?"

Arnhardt moved his body very slightly yet it had the effect of a significant effort on the part of a ponderous and unwieldy mass.

"There have been three murders committed here as well as an attempted murder. No one's going to leave until they're cleared up."

Flores' laugh rang out clearly, its taunt unconcealed. Only his eyes, Rennert saw, lacked confidence. They were sharp and wary.

"That promises to be a lengthy process, Mr. Arnhardt. And even in this out-of-the-way place one man—even a citizen of the great United States—cannot stand at the door with a loaded gun for twenty-four hours out of the day. It must end sometime. And when it does the authorities of my country may have questions to ask. Very unpleasant questions, Mr. Arnhardt."

"They can ask 'em today if they want to. I'm going down to Victoria and bring them up here."

Flores' teeth flashed in another wider smile.

"Excellent, Mr. Arnhardt! Excellent! I shall be most pleased to renew acquaintance with my father's cousin, who is commandant of the federal troops stationed there. You must ask for him in particular. He will consider it a slight on the dignity of his position if you do not. Gaspar Flores y Montes his name is. Be sure and remember it."

Arnhardt's fingers had separated themselves from the butt of the gun and his hand lay inertly on the tablecloth. Rennert was reminded of a young and harassed bull in the ring when it first discovers that its ponderous strength cannot stop the sharp *banderillas* that sting it each time it charges the red cape flaunted before its eyes.

Some of Flores' suavity vanished and his voice had the needle sharpness of the dowels: "Don Gaspar will ask you perhaps why you have delayed so long in calling in the authorities. Why you have waited until your partner, Mr. Falter, is dead. Why you said nothing when your stepfather, Mr. Stahl, died here and left you his interest in this hacienda. What, in fact, you intend doing with this hacienda—so isolated, so far from the watchful eyes of the authorities."

Rennert thought for a moment that Arnhardt was going to lunge across the table at the Mexican. His jaw was thrust out and the cords of his neck were thick straight ridges. His fingers were pulling the tablecloth toward him. He got to his feet, reached out for the gun and thrust it into his hip pocket. He stood for a moment in indecision, his baffled eyes fixed on the tablecloth.

Flores' voice came again, a little less sharp and slower: "Don Gaspar will understand about the shot that was fired at you last night. He is of the old school and still believes that a man should protect his honor. He will doubtless lecture the husband who fired the shot on the poorness of his aim. That is all."

"God damn you!" Arnhardt lowered his head and made for the door. He jerked it open and left it swinging furiously in the wind.

Flores' laugh was an ineffectual attempt to maintain bravado.

"I trust that I shall see you again before I leave, Mr. Rennert." He got up and his voice was none too steady. "At lunch, I expect, since this storm will probably last until afternoon."

Rennert said: "You have given up your search?"

Flores was folding his napkin with careful deliberate fingers.

"Yes, Mr. Rennert, I have given it up as hopeless. Too much time has passed."

"Then you have not found what you were looking for?"

"No, I have not found the body of my grandfather.

"I wasn't referring to the body of your grandfather, Mr. Flores."

The thin sensitive fingers were very still on the folds of the white cloth. Very still and stiff, with their tips pressed down firmly.

"I do not understand you, Mr. Rennert."

"I think that you do. One does not look for a dead body with a divining-rod."

The fingers moved, unfolded the napkin and began to crease it again unsteadily.

"You know then, Mr. Rennert?"

"Yes."

"And how did you know? Miss Fahn told you?"

"No, she thought the instrument you had was a telescope. I knew that it was something else when I saw how eager you were to impress upon me the story of your grandfather. A few minutes ago I saw the instrument. I don't know just how it is supposed to work but I judge that you bought it as an improvement on the old-fashioned witch hazel twig."

"Yes, they said that it would do away with the vibrations that came from contact with the human hand. That it was infallible."

"And you found that it isn't?"

"Last night I made a test, something which I had not thought of before. I laid a thermometer on the floor, close to the instrument. The divinometer, it's called. There was no response, even when I put the mercury directly under the wood."

Rennert felt a little sorry for the discouragement in the tone. He said: "You are fortunate that you were disillusioned this early. Many men here in Mexico have spent their entire lives in the same search and have died finding nothing. What was it—buried treasure or a gold mine?"

"The family plate and jewels, Mr. Rennert. My father took only a part of them to the United States. The rest were hidden by my grandfather. They were never found. I do not think now that they will ever be found."

Rennert remembered Conrad's men on Azuera, men that could not die once treasure had fastened upon their minds. "You are determined to leave as soon as the storm stops?" he asked

"Yes, Mr. Rennert"

"My advice would be," Rennert said with low emphasis, "to wait. I hope that you aren't discounting Mr. Arnhardt and his gun." The deadly suspense of this enforced waiting for that overt move that must come sooner or later. The strain of keeping smoothed with oil the deceptively placid surface that at any moment might rebel and loose undercurrents fraught with danger.

"I believe," the Mexican said slowly, "that I have Mr. Arnhardt checkmated."

"I wouldn't be too sure. A bullet is a play to which there is usually no answering move."

"I know." The olive face was suddenly serious. "You have seen a young bull—a *novillo*—in the ring? Sometimes he will get in one position, with his back to the wall as it were, and refuse to budge. His *querencia*, we call it. He is most dangerous then," he said as he let the napkin rest on the table.

28
LULL

ANN TOLMAN STOOD under the shelter of the eaves on the other side of the archway and looked into the pounding rain that was a solid slanting wall between her and the dining-room door. She lowered her head and plunged resolutely into it. Her feet slipped in the gray-yellow water that swirled over the stones, she righted herself and came to the door where Rennert stood.

She stopped beside him and shook her drenched hair.

"Isn't this glorious!" her voice rose vibrantly above the crashing of the rain and the steady whining drone of the wind. "I feel as if all the cobwebs were being washed out of my brain."

"It *is* a grand spectacle," Rennert agreed, studying her face. "I was looking at those clouds a few minutes ago and thinking how appropriately the Norsemen imagined them to be Valkyries, the beautiful—and deadly—daughters of Odin."

She raised her head. A subtle yet distinct change had come over her. Her wet face retained its white look but beneath its plane of ice something glowed, reflecting itself in her eyes, bright with a fire that he had not seen there before. After a moment a tremor ran over her shoulders.

"I was forgetting about the danger. I suppose, though, that things are always more beautiful when they're not quite safe."

"At the risk of being trite, the moth and the flame, of course."

She stared into the rain for a long time without speaking. Then her lips set firmly, she turned her head and glanced into the dining room.

"I'd like to have a cup of coffee." She looked back at him. "If you have a few minutes to spare, why don't you come in while I drink it?"

He followed her in and rang for Lee. There was an interval of silence while the coffee was being brought. He offered her a cigarette. She took it and held it to his match without seeming to be aware of what she was doing. She leaned forward and her eyes met his steadily.

"Mr. Rennert, who shot Mark Arnhardt last night?"

"I'm being perfectly frank with you, Mrs. Tolman. I'm not yet sure."

"You don't think Steve did it then?"

"I don't think he did."

She smiled and some of the color began to come back into her cheeks.

"You've relieved my mind! I was afraid, you see, of what you were going to say. Because," she stated emphatically, "Steve *didn't* do it. He wouldn't explain about the gun but I'm going to. You have to know something about him before you understand why he took the gun and why he wouldn't explain."

She paused and took a long sip of the coffee.

"Steve," she said as she set the cup down, "has been unfortunate all his life. He was left an orphan when he was very young and was brought up by a maiden aunt. He spent his boyhood in an atmosphere of overstuffed chairs, antimacassars and gilt portraits. You understand what I mean?"

"I think I understand perfectly, Mrs. Tolman."

"Instead of letting his emotions flow out in the ordinary channels, like other boys, he kept them bottled up inside him. An introvert, I suppose you'd call him. His first year or two at college were terribly unhappy ones. He didn't fit in. That's when I first knew him. I suppose it was one of the first things that attracted me to him. He began gradually to become more expansive. I think I was mostly responsible for that. By the time we were married he had almost become his normal self. Then came the tuberculosis."

She stared for a long time into the smoke. She was looking, Rennert knew, not at it but back into the years. She drained the coffee cup and went on.

"At first I didn't understand his attitude about that. His attitude toward me, too. He became cold and reserved, sort of shrunk inside himself. I realized finally what the trouble was. He resented what he thought was my pity. His feeling must have begun long before, when he had first known me. I had probably made it worse by being so obvious about my efforts to help him adjust himself to college life. I was responsible for his getting into a fraternity, for example. The success of his efforts to adjust himself must have come from a determination to stand on his own feet, without any need of help from me. When he found he had tuberculosis all the emotional constrictions that he had almost gotten rid of came back on him with greater force than ever. He thought of himself as helpless, obliged to stand by while I dashed about energetically trying to arrange things for both of us. Then we came down here. Things reached their nadir. The long hot days with nothing to do but just exist. And Mark Arnhardt was here."

She crushed the stub of the cigarette into the saucer, her fingers moving it about in slow concentric circles.

"I suppose there is a great contrast between Mark and Steve, although I didn't realize it at first. Physically, I mean. Emotionally, I don't know that they're so different. I liked Mark very much, somewhat the way one likes a big Newfoundland dog that doesn't know what to do with all his energies. We got into the habit of taking walks over the mountains, going hunting together, things like that. I don't think I could have stood it if it hadn't been for Mark. And all the time Steve had to spend the long afternoons in bed, staring out at the sunlight and thinking of Mark's strong legs taking him over the rocks. The idea of suicide must have come to him then. He would step out of the picture, Mark and I would get married and everything would be straightened out."

"And his feelings toward Arnhardt?" Rennert asked. "What were they?"

She stared down with a frown of concentration.

"I think," she said slowly, "that he always liked Mark, would have been glad to become friendly with him. He felt, though, that there wasn't any use in making the attempt. Mark was so strong and healthy, representing everything that he wasn't. He was jealous of him, too, probably without realizing it. Not at first, at least, on account of me but on account of his strength."

"Did he realize the meaning of the episode in the patio yesterday afternoon?"

"Yes, he guessed what I had attempted to do but he put the wrong interpretation on it. Typical of him. He thought that I was in despair because I couldn't marry Mark. To him it was proof of how much I cared for Mark. So he decided to take the step that he had been contemplating for a long time. He got the gun from Falter's desk and was going to shoot himself during the night."

"While I was with him he watched you and Arnhardt standing in the door."

"Yes, I know. The flower that I put in Mark's buttonhole. He told me about it. It was so foolish of him but it's little things like that which cause the greatest tragedies, I suppose. If you hadn't found that gun last night he wouldn't be alive this morning."

She stopped and her eyes went quickly to the window. She looked back at him.

"That was so sudden. It almost startled me. The stopping of the wind."

There was something startling about the abrupt cessation of the whine and scream and about the stillness which with its cessation impressed itself sharply on the room. It was the unexpected loss of power of a dynamo. The rain was no longer a wall of water shattering over their heads but had sunk to a steady even shower that pattered monotonously on the tiles, emphasizing the utter silence of the wind.

Her voice sounded strangely loud and strained: "There's one thing I haven't been able to understand, though. That's Mark's attitude toward Steve. He never mentions him when we are alone. Seems to shy away from any reference to him, in fact. When they are together he acts stiff and formal and self. conscious. Yet I've always had the feeling that he liked Steve."

"I think I can explain part of his attitude. Arnhardt has always suspected your husband of poisoning his stepfather."

She stared at him incredulously.

"But why?"

"Because of what took place in San Antonio. He admitted to me that he wouldn't have blamed Mr. Tolman for feeling that he had been wronged. I think you're right as to his liking for him. He was reluctant to admit to himself that he did suspect him. Then, too, his friendship with you put him in an awkward position. If he had brought charges against your husband, well, you see how it would have looked."

She said in a low voice: "David and the woman of Bathsheba?"

"Yes."

She seemed lost for several moments in her thoughts. When she raised her eyes there was a telltale brightness in them.

"But that doesn't solve our problem, does it? Someone did shoot Mark." There was a distinct hardening of her face and of her voice. "I'm going to tell you something now that I've hesitated to do before. I never thought that it might have any importance until last night. Besides, it's rather embarrassing for me to speak of it. It's about Esteban Flores." She hesitated and looked at him with a weak smile. "I wonder if you'd let me have another cigarette? I quit smoking them because Steve can't. I feel now that I have to have them in order to keep going. There's something uncanny about this stillness. It's more nerve-racking than the wind. I'm sure I owe you at least a package."

"Quite all right, Mrs. Tolman." Rennert held out a light. "It's merely a lull, you know, before the rest of the storm." He lit one for himself and said: "You were speaking of Mr. Flores."

"Yes," she inhaled deeply and leaned back in her chair. "When he first came here he made things very difficult for me. I suppose it's the Mexican attitude toward women but I wasn't used to it. From the very first time I met him he seemed to take it for granted that I was ready to enter into an affair with him. Nothing that I could take offense at particularly. Just a way he had of looking at me and of addressing me. He would come to the room when he knew Steve wasn't there and bring me presents—flowers and things. I tried to show him my indifference to him without hurting his feelings but it didn't do any good. He kept persisting. One evening, just about dusk, while we were in the patio, he tried to kiss me. I just laughed at him." Her eyes were frank. "I've found that's the most effective way of getting out of such a situation. Much better than dramatics."

"And since?" Rennert asked when he saw that she seemed reluctant to continue.

"He has never made another attempt to approach me. I don't know whether it was my ridicule or whether someone—Mark or Steve—saw us and did something. The next day, however, Mark was morose and silent. Esteban stayed in his room all day. When I saw him next he had—well, he had a black eye. I suppose if I hadn't had a sense of humor I would have gotten romantic and thought of myself as the fair lady for whom two men did battle. But since Miss Fahn, Maria, and I were the only women on the place it didn't flatter my vanity to any extent. It just amused me. Now," the lightness dropped from her manner and her eyes were troubled as they sought the window, "I don't know. It may have been more serious than I thought."

Rennert was silent for a moment.

"Have you seen since then any indications that Flores—to use a venerable expression—harbored a grudge against Arnhardt?"

"I don't know whether you'd call it that or not. It's so hard to tell what Esteban is thinking. I've noticed, though, that he always takes an almost diabolical delight in making sport of Mark when someone else is present. Little innuendoes that for the most part go over Mark's head. Mark knows that they are going over his head, though, and that makes him furious. Maybe I shouldn't have told you all this but I thought you ought to know about everything. I haven't any compunctions about keeping still when it's a question of Steve's safety. And whoever shot Mark last night must have seen us in the doorway. Must have seen him leave and shot him." She got up. "I hope, Mr. Rennert, that you won't think I've been posing as a *femme fatale*. I know my limitations, I assure you. But you *will* try to prove that Steve is innocent of all this?"

"Yes, Mrs. Tolman." Rennert too rose. "I shall do my best."

"Thank you." She paused halfway to the door. "I wish that you would go and comfort Miss Fahn. I think you and I are the only ones here whom she really trusts."

"Very well. Again I'll promise to do my best."

The patio was a place of wreckage. Torn petals and leaves were strewn about over the paths and paving-stones. Here and there they were heaped in little windrows, as if dropped suddenly by a hand. The rain had almost ceased but the lid of the sky seemed to have come closer under the weight of the heavy rolling clouds. The silence was unreal and sinister to ears accustomed for hours to the screaming of the wind.

Rennert stopped by his room, then knocked at Miss Fahn's door. He saw her peer furtively through the window. In a moment she opened the door and stood behind it as he entered. She closed it and locked and bolted it.

"I just wanted to be sure, Mr. Rennert," she said again.

She was a part of the dimness of the room and of the pallid grayness that veiled the windows. She seemed to have aged incredibly during the night. Her face was like putty hanging in loose flaccid folds under her haggard old eyes and about her drawn lips.

Rennert laid a package upon the table.

"Here is your dissertation," he said with a joviality which he was far from feeling. "Thank you very much."

"Oh, yes." She seemed dazed, unable for a moment to center her attention on him. "Do you have a car, Mr. Rennert?"

"Yes, Miss Fahn."

She came a step closer and he could hear her labored breathing. She clasped her hands together and nervously rubbed their palms.

"Will you take me in to Victoria or some place? This morning. Right away. I must get away from this terrible place."

"I think it would be better to wait until later, Miss Fahn. The storm, you know, is not over yet."

"Not over?" She had to steady herself with a hand on the table. "But it is! The wind has stopped blowing."

"I don't want to alarm you but I'm afraid it's only a lull and that the wind will begin again soon, stronger than ever. We are perfectly safe within these walls but I shouldn't like to venture out into the open in a car."

She sank onto the edge of the bed and stared out the window. Her hands were twitching.

"Oh, Mr. Rennert, I'd rather be out in the storm. Any place but here. If only Mr. Flores' plane were in order! Maybe he would take me away. I'm afraid! Afraid to eat or drink anything! Afraid to open the door! With a murderer loose—"

Rennert felt pity surge through him. He thought: *The terrible thing about excessive unrestrained fear is that it borders inevitably on the ludicrous.*

Then he heard it edging louder through the electrically charged stillness.

The hum of an airplane.

29
THE STIR OF A LEAF

THE SKY PRESSED close, smoothed now of some of its clouds. Those that remained, in the south, were darker, their gray edges tinged with saffron as they seethed in rolling, turbulent confusion, checked in their northward advance.

The stillness persisted.

Rennert walked out of the hacienda, his eyes searching the sky and the open ground.

Flores' plane stood as the day before, its wings a tarnished gray against a grayer backdrop. His conjecture when the drone of a plane had come to him in Miss Fahn's room had been correct. Flores was in the house.

He walked past the yucca tree.

A faint "Hallo" came to his ears, echoing weirdly in the still air compounded by the cliffs. He turned to his left, in the direction of the sound. A man was coming around a rocky spur that sloped sharply onto the flat tableland on which the hacienda stood.

It was Edward Solier.

Rennert waved a hand and advanced to meet him. Solier came forward a few yards, slowly, then stopped and sat upon a rock that had fallen from the declivity above.

As Rennert came closer, he got up and his voice rang out clearly: "Good morning, Mr. Rennert."

"Good morning. Glad to see you."

"I seem to have picked the worst morning possible for my trip."

"Yes." Rennert stepped up and they shook hands.

Solier wore whipcord breeches, a leather jacket and a flying-helmet. They served to dwarf his slight body. His face looked drawn and tired but his voice held an undercurrent of suppressed excitement and his eyes were feverishly bright.

"If I'd waited a couple of hours the storm would have been over. I thought for a few minutes I wasn't going to make it. The first time in my life I was really frightened. I landed the plane in a little open space between two ridges back there. A natural landing place I always use. It's safer than coming too close to the house." He gestured backward with his head. "Suppose we sit down here somewhere and talk a few minutes. We'll have more privacy than at the house. I'd hoped I could get in touch with you before I put in an appearance there."

"All right."

They rounded the rocky projection and came onto a flat space bare of rocks and trees. The plane stood in the center, its nose pointed toward a wide gap in the cliffs. They sat down on a ledge and Solier removed the helmet and jacket, laying them beside him.

"Now," he leaned back and crossed his legs, "tell me what the situation is here at the hacienda, Rennert."

Rennert held one foot propped against the stone. His right arm was about his knee as he regarded Solier through the smoke of the cigarette which he held in his left hand.

"When I accepted your proposal in San Antonio," he said slowly, "I didn't expect that it would turn out to be as grim and unpleasant a business as it has. If I had I should have thought twice and refused it. The past sixteen hours have been hectic ones."

"So I judged from my conversation with you last night." Solier held his head forward, his eyes moving quickly over Rennert's face as if seeking to read there what he was about to say. "What's happened since then?"

Rennert was deliberate.

"You will have to pardon me if I go at my narrative in what seems an odd way. There are so many different threads running through this case that it's important to keep them separate." He was formulating his own thoughts, as he spoke, separating these threads for his own benefit as much as Solier's. "You asked me to do two things for you. First, to learn what was becoming of the water."

"Yes." There was a note of impatience in Solier's voice.

"I have done that. It was the easiest part of the puzzle—"

"Who was taking it?" Solier broke in.

"Maria Montemayor. The natural love of flowers that one finds universally in Mexico was in her case intensified to what amounted to an all-absorbing passion, particularly after her only son died and was buried under them. When the springs in the mountains began to dry up she saw the flowers drying up and took a course that to her seemed perfectly justified. She took the drinking-water from the kitchen and gave it to the flowers. She was helped by the fact that Lee, who had charge of the kitchen, was away for a time. Twice that I know of, once before he left and again last night, she resorted to a device for keeping him from hearing her when she was getting the water. She left *marihuana* cigarettes in his room. He smoked them, got on a jag and was soon asleep for the rest of the night."

"Well!" it was a colorless interjection. Solier had been tapping his fingers restlessly upon the rock while Rennert was speaking. "Maria's been on the place so long that I suppose she thinks she almost owns it. Go ahead," he said, "the water's not so important."

"I realize that, Mr. Solier. Remember that I'm merely getting rid of some of the aspects of the case that added to the complication of it. I think that you will I see when I am through that the more serious aspect is rather clear cut."

"You mean Miguel's death?"

"Mr. Falter has died too. Early this morning."

"He has?" Solier was silent, his lips indrawn.

"I am referring also to George Stahl's death," Rennert said. "But you will remember that my mission down here had nothing to do with murder at the beginning. I have cleared up the matter of the water. Now, as to my other errand, here is Miss Fahn's receipt for the money paid her for her shares and her release of them." He brought the papers out of his pocket and passed them to Solier.

The latter took them, gave them a cursory glance and thrust them inside his coat.

"Fine." He looked at Rennert expectantly.

Rennert did not continue for a long time. There was a look of abstraction on his face as he stared past Solier's sharp profile, past the receding vastnesses of the mountains, into the clouds restive in restraint on the southwestern horizon.

"What's the matter with you, Rennert?" Solier asked sharply. "You act as if you didn't want to go ahead. All this talk about the water and Miss Fahn's shares could have waited until later. You spoke over the radio as if you were certain that murder had been committed here. That's why I came down. Are you still of that opinion or have I come on a wild-goose chase?"

"I'm certain—without a shadow of a doubt. Deliberate planned murder." Was he mistaken or *had* he seen a gentle stirring of a leaf in the petrified vegetation of that slope?

"Do you know the identity of the murderer?"

Solier's features were transferred as if by other-dimensional means to a flaw in the rocks straight ahead of Rennert's eyes. There was in the fractured stone a distinct resemblance to his aquiline nose, his pointed chin, his jutting eyebrows. The mobility which had marked them in that San Antonio office was mostly gone now and they had some of the hard insensitivity of the rock.

"Yes," Rennert said, "I know the identity of the murderer."

"Who is it? Mark Arnhardt?" Sharply, as no reply was forthcoming: "You don't want to reveal it?"

A grim smile stole over Rennert's face. (His eyes must have been at fault. The blades of grass were motionless against the sky.)

"No," he said, "it's not that. I promise to tell you the name before our conversation is over. But there are one or two things that must be cleared up first, in order to make the case complete against this person. I'm going to ask you a direct question. I hope that you will answer me frankly. What was your company's real purpose in buying this hacienda?"

Very distinct was the scraping of Solier's nails on the surface of the rock as he suddenly contracted his fingers. As he stared at

Rennert his face took on a rigidity that matched perfectly that of the stone beyond him. It was a full minute before he spoke.

"What are your reasons for thinking the purpose wasn't as I told you—to build a hotel?"

"Several, Mr. Solier. I got a hint of it in our first conversation. From the amount you offered me to come down here I suspected that something more important than an abandoned plan for a hotel was at stake. Then there was the question of the amount you paid for this property. You stated that there was a great deal of land about here to be had almost for the asking. Yet you spoke of paying the Flores family a big price. When I pointed out this inconsistency, you may remember, you countered by saying that they had held you up because of their knowledge that the road was to come through here. I have learned since that it was not a large amount you paid. A very small one, in fact, when one considers the extent of this land. Is that correct?"

"Yes." Solier shrugged in defeat. "That's right. I'm going to be frank with you, Rennert. You're enough of a business man to realize how these things have to be managed. We paid the Flores family as little as we could. Ten thousand *pesos*. On our statement to the stockholders it appeared as," he paused and cleared his throat, "slightly larger. When the plan for the hotel had to be given up we told the stockholders that we had spent a lot of capital and couldn't pay them the full amount on their shares. We made a little profit out of it, yes, but it's done every day in business like this."

"And your company retained possession of the hacienda with the exception of Miss Fahn's shares?"

"Yes."

"And when Miss Fahn could be persuaded to sell those you and Falter and Stahl—and later Arnhardt—would have entire control of this property away from direct contact with the world, yet near enough that automobiles from Monterrey and other cities in this section of Mexico could reach it easily—and in privacy?"

"Yes," Solier nodded, his eyes narrowing slightly.

"My suspicion that there was more behind the deal than appeared on the surface was strengthened when I found that a power

plant had been installed recently. Last night I saw the plans that
Stephen Tolman drew for your so-called hotel. The hotel appearance on the first and second floors to divert suspicion. The large
room on the third floor, glass-roofed, for gambling tables."

30
ORDEAL BY WIND

THE SILENCE BETWEEN the two men lengthened while a faint rustling crept at them. No object on the landscape betrayed the source of the almost imperceptible sound yet there was everywhere a soft stir as of invisible things in the coarse grasses marching ant-like forward.

Solier laughed brittlely.

"All right," he said resignedly, "you've got the dope on us. It *was* a gambling casino we had in mind from the beginning. A great opportunity, you'll admit. Close to Monterrey and Brownsville and the Pan-American Highway. It would attract people from all the border cities, especially since this new administration has been closing down most of the places along the border. We rigged up this scheme among us—to form a company and sell shares for a hotel before it was known generally just where the highway would go."

"You knew yourselves of course?"

"Oh, yes. Everything worked out as we had planned. As soon as the route of the highway was laid out we told our stockholders that the deal was off and that we had spent most of their money on the land. They all turned their shares in for whatever we gave them. Except Miss Fahn. If she had stayed in Austin we could have gone ahead anyway and built the casino. But what did the damned woman do but decide to come down here and study plants! We sized her up and figured that she'd screech to high heaven if she found out she was mixed up in a gambling scheme. The Mexican authorities would get wind of it and everything would go up in smoke. So

179

it was necessary to get her shares before she suspected what was up. We were at a standstill, you see."

"I'm still wondering why you chose me for the errand."

Solier laughed drily.

"Well, Rennert, to tell you the truth you fitted the bill perfectly. A pleasant middle-aged man who would inspire confidence in a maiden lady. Good manners, something she is a stickler for. An official position that would serve as a sort of voucher for you and offset in a way your temporary connection with Falter and me, whom she looked on a little askance. Your work," he patted his pocket, "proves that I was right."

"So," Rennert said, "we have the set-up at the time I came here. A large amount of money already invested at stake and a still larger amount in prospect for the person or persons who owned the place. A motive sufficient for murder."

Solier's eyes were steel-hard; they darkened as he drew his eyebrows into a frown.

"Correct!" His voice was crisp. "The motive. And now the murderer."

"I am ready now," Rennert said, "to go back and begin a chronological account of my visit here. As I told you, I found when I arrived yesterday afternoon that Miguel Montemayor had been taken ill a few hours before. Soon after drinking whisky from a bottle in the wardrobe of the room to which Falter assigned me. That whisky was, I am sure, intended for me. It was expected that I would find it and, since only a small amount remained, drink all of it, leaving no evidence that it had been poisoned. The murderer, then, knew that I was to have that room."

(A leaf stirred, then another. It was in the trailing milk vetch that it was first visible. The silvery leaves were stirring and the racemes of deep purple flowers were moving gently to and fro in an effort to contort their heads northward.)

"Soon after I arrived," a quickening could have been discerned in Rennert's voice, "Mr. Falter fell sick. He had been complaining of stomach trouble for some time, I knew. If it had not been for the coincidence of Miguel's illness I might not have suspected the presence of poison. The symptoms were the same, however, particularly the yellow vision which I mentioned to you over the radio. In Miguel's case it was associated with yellow flowers, the Mexican death symbol. I played for a time with the idea that the secret might lie somewhere in this association of these particular flowers and death. George Stahl, too, had died on the hacienda after a stroke in which he had fallen among yellow flowers and had talked incoherently about things being yellow. But when Falter fell prostrate at the dinner table after objects had become yellow for him I decided that I was doing as Miguel had done and was concentrating my attention on yellow flowers instead of the color yellow."

(It was unmistakable now—the air that washed his face in ever stronger flood and weaker ebb. His watch ticked excitedly, warningly.)

"I next asked myself how the poison had been administered to Falter. Judging by the quickness with which it took effect in Miguel's case I decided that it must have been given after or soon before my arrival. Upon questioning Falter I found that he had eaten or drunk nothing since lunch except some whisky and those tablets which you sent down to him by me. I had drunk out of the same whisky bottle. Therefore the poison must have been put into the tablets." Rennert paused. "By the way, I notice that you didn't bring a doctor with you."

"No." Solier's attention seemed to have wandered. "I couldn't get one to come so far."

"Did you learn anything about what the poison may have been?"

"No."

"I did."

"Yes? What was it?"

"It was after my last conversation with you last night that I recalled a conversation I once had with a doctor. This identified the poison. Santonin. He had mentioned a case in which an overdose had been given as a vermifuge and the patient had died after showing symptoms of yellow vision. My first thought was that the murderer had obtained it in its natural state somewhere about here since it comes from a plant known as wormseed or Mexican tea. I found that I was on a cold trail, there, however. A son of Miguel and Maria died this spring of worms, I learned. The doctor who attended him left a quantity of medicine here. That medicine must have been santonin. The murderer must have learned of its use at that time since he used a portion of this santonin to poison George Stahl soon after."

Solier had sat up, holding himself very tense as he regarded Rennert.

"So, Mr. Solier, I had the poison identified and the motive. They led me to the murderer. Now, if you will pardon my injection of business into this, I want to ask you this: have I or have I not fulfilled my mission here?"

Solier frowned.

"Why, yes, Rennert, you have," he said hesitantly. "Why?"

"Because I want to straighten out our business arrangement before I go any further. I should appreciate it if you would pay me now the amount you promised me for my services."

The frown deepened.

"Well, if you say so," there was definite coolness in the voice. "It's a bit irregular, of course, but I have no objections."

"If you will then, Mr. Solier."

"Very well. I brought some cash down with me. I think there's enough. Oh, I see I left my brief-case in the plane. Wait a minute and I'll get it." He rose and walked away.

Rennert sat and watched him. He leaned back on the rock comfortably and let his arm rest on Solier's jacket. The thick fleece lining was very soft on his moving fingers until they suddenly came to rest on a hard object.

He felt terribly diminutive, terribly insignificant as he stared at the sky and thought: *Have I the sublime egoism to assume the role which I am about to assume?*

When Solier returned he was in the same position. The introspective look which had clouded his eyes was gone, leaving them clear and unwavering.

Solier handed him a roll of bills held together by a rubber band.

"You think," he said as he sat down, "that I might refuse to pay you if you told me the name of the murderer first?"

"Thank you, Mr. Solier." Rennert slipped the bills into a wallet. "That is exactly what I was afraid of." He shifted his position slightly, turning to face Solier. His voice was no longer deliberate. "I was speaking a moment ago of the motive. You realize what it was, of course. Last night Mark Arnhardt was fired on and wounded. Regarding Miguel's death as a miscarriage of the murderer's plans, that leaves Stahl, Falter, and Arnhardt whom the murderer had undertaken to remove. All of them men who owned interests in this hacienda."

"I suspected as much. That's the reason I was afraid to come down myself. I was afraid that I would be next."

Rennert's eyes went to the sky, where banked clouds were piling in dangerous top-heaviness, then back to Solier's face.

"Wasn't the real reason you sent me down here to provide yourself with an alibi, Mr. Solier? So that Mr. Falter would be poisoned while you sat in an office in San Antonio?"

Solier leaned back on the jacket, his fingers plucking at the wool of its lining.

"Go ahead, Mr. Rennert," his voice was perfectly level.

"It was you, Mr. Solier, who poisoned those tablets. But in San Antonio, not after they were brought here to the hacienda. It was you who left the poisoned whisky in the room which you occupied while here. The room which you left locked and which you instructed Falter to put me into. The plan must have been germinating in your mind for a long time. It was a very well-thought-out move. I would give Falter the tablets soon after my arrival since he was anxious to get them and would ask for them at once. He would take them, I would drink the whisky and both of us would fall ill and die. There would be nothing to connect you with our deaths. You would come down, bring the attention of the authorities to the matter and point out that of all the people present at the hacienda at the time of our deaths Arnhardt alone profited. You would probably have accounted for my death by saying that I had detected

Arnhardt's guilt and that he had to put me out of the way for safety. Wasn't that it, Mr. Solier?"

Still the even, emotionless voice: "Go ahead, Mr. Rennert. You're interesting me very much."

Rennert went on: "I unintentionally forced your hand by telling you that Arnhardt suspected someone of poisoning his stepfather and that he had given me information as to this person's guilt. You were afraid that you were the one he had in mind. You flew down here yesterday evening after our last radio conversation, while there was still light. You landed at a distance from the house and waited until dark. You entered the patio then and at the first opportunity shot Arnhardt. Your footsteps were heard by two people, by the way, when you ran back to your plane. This morning you rose from the ground, circled around and came down here, as if you had just arrived from San Antonio. You know you could not have flown south this morning directly in the face of that wind."

Solier moved again, propping himself on an elbow with one hand buried under the jacket. His face was wooden.

"Really, Mr. Rennert, I didn't credit you with so much imagination. I suppose you have thought about proof for this cock-and-bull theory of yours?"

"Certainly. I realize that the evidence I have just pointed out is mostly circumstantial. The matter of the fingerprints wouldn't be so easily explained away."

"Fingerprints?" Interest ruffled the surface of Solier's voice.

"Yes, when you put the santonin in those caramels of Stahl's you left, unfortunately, a very clear impression of your fingerprints on one piece that Stahl did not eat. They are not those of any of the individuals on the hacienda. It will not require the services of an expert to prove that they are yours. Shall we go to the house now and make the test?" He made a motion as if to rise.

Solier's hand was steadied by his elbow on the stone and it held the muzzle of the pistol pointed straight at the pit of Rennert's stomach.

"You are not only imaginative, Rennert, but foolish as well. Do you realize that there's nothing on earth to stop me from shooting you, getting in my plane and leaving? No one has witnessed our little meeting. By the time you are missed and your body found I shall be well on my way back to San Antonio. It will be just another mysterious death. Bandits, I suppose, will be blamed for it."

Rennert looked at the automatic.

"A Colt forty-five, I believe?" he asked.

"Yes."

"The same gun with which you shot Arnhardt last night?"

"Since you want to know, yes." There was no relaxation of the steadiness of the eyes and hand.

"Since this is a moment for confidences, I worked out the case correctly, didn't I?" Rennert started to put a hand into his pocket for cigarettes. Solier stopped him with a gesture.

"Keep your hands where they are, Rennert, or I'll send a bullet into your belly. If it will flatter your vanity to know it, you got everything correct."

"Well, then," Rennert stood up, feeling wind slap his face, "you'd better get in your plane first, hadn't you? You will want to get under way immediately in case the shot is heard at the house and someone takes a notion to investigate."

A puzzled look came into Solier's eyes. He caught up his jacket and helmet with one hand and backed toward the plane, keeping Rennert covered with the automatic.

"Come twist the propeller." He spoke between set teeth.

Rennert regarded him, smiling pleasantly. "Really, Mr. Solier, that's a great favor to ask of a man whom you are going to kill in just a moment. Suppose I should refuse?"

There was a vicious glint in Solier's eyes.

"I'd do this," his voice was deadly soft. "I'd shoot you once or perhaps twice in spots that wouldn't be fatal but that would be very painful. I'd turn the propeller myself then, leisurely. When I got ready to go I'd end your suffering."

Rennert shrugged.

"You win. I've seen men with bullets in their stomachs. It's not a pleasant sight. I'll turn your propeller for you to the best of my ability."

"Then hurry up."

"It's customary, I believe, here in Mexico to let a man die with a cigarette between his lips. I am an inveterate cigarette smoker. May I light one?"

Solier hesitated, his eyes narrowing in suspicion.

"Go ahead," he said. "I noticed that you didn't have a gun on you."

Rennert took cigarettes from his pocket, selected one and lit it without haste. He flipped the match away and said: "All right, thanks. Let's go."

Solier moved cautiously toward the plane. Rennert followed him, inhaling smoke, and watched him get in. He walked toward the propeller then, twirled it and stood back. The whir of the blades mingled with a low distant rumble that wasn't, he knew, that of any machine made by man.

Solier did not seem to hear it. He leaned over the side of the plane, leveled the automatic directly at Rennert's stomach and pulled the trigger.

Rennert's voice rose over the drone: "I forgot to tell you, Mr. Solier, that I removed the cartridges from that gun while you were getting that money from the plane."

Solier's words were inaudible. The plane shot forward, passed with precision between the walls of rock and rose gracefully into the air. It circled and headed north.

Rennert stood for a moment, watching it, then started to walk back to the hacienda. He felt himself pushed forward and heard the stampeding thunder of rain on the ground behind him. He quickened his steps, broke into a run. Before he had gained the shelter of the adobe walls the wind struck him, almost felling him with the violence of its impact. Water lashed and choked him.

He reached the doorway, paused there gasping for breath then edged his way along the walls to the north side of the house. He stood, crouched in refuge from the wind and the sheets of wind-driven rain, and watched Solier's plane.

It was a blotch on the sky the size of a desert eagle, beginning to climb higher, when the wind hit it. He saw it waver, erratically renew its ascent, remain apparently motionless for a second or so, then dip to one side and spin toward the unbroken mountain tops.

He was cold, as if the wind that shook the walls at his back were crested with ice.

It wasn't a pleasant way to send a man to his death.

31
AFTERMATH

THE RAYS OF THE SUN were brittle-dear in the clean-washed air of morning. The sky was innocent and guileless, of soft blue silk dappled with white clouds that dazzled the eye. Vapors were beginning to rise like mirages from the wet ground, battered by the wind and rain that had persisted in undiminished fury for most of the previous day. By the middle of the afternoon the storm had begun to slacken and at sunset had ceased in exhaustion.

Rennert stood with one foot on the running-board of his car and stared at the ramparts of rock to the north. He said to the elderly, inattentive Mexican officer who stood beside him, immaculate in uniform and gold braid: "I have given you as nearly as I can the location of the spot where the plane crashed. It will be very difficult to locate it in those mountains, I am afraid."

Captain Gaspar Flores y Montes waved this aside with a manicured hand.

"Do not think of that, Mr. Rennert. I shall send a searching party today or tomorrow or, since that is a holiday in our state, the next day. They will try to find the plane. And if not?" He shrugged. "The mountains hold many secrets. They can hold one more." The hand stayed in the air, including in its comprehensive sweep the adobe walls, the stone pillars of the gateway, the mountains even. "The duty which brought me here, Mr. Rennert, has become a pleasure. I am filled with happiness to see this hacienda again, to draw the odor of its soil into my lungs," he breathed deeply if a bit asthmatically, "to be again with my young cousin in the place where

188

our ancestors lived for so many generations. Perhaps some day the Flores family will come again into possession of this, its birthplace." He let emotion simmer a moment then turned to Rennert. "This young countryman of yours, this Mr. Arnhardt, is now the sole owner of the hacienda, is he not?"

"Yes, Captain Flores."

"And he should be willing to sell, should he not? After these regrettable experiences here."

"I could not say. You might approach him on the subject."

"I shall do it! I shall do it! I have a daughter. The father of Esteban has hinted at marriage. I shall buy this hacienda back into the family. It shall be my wedding present to the young couple. There will be a fiesta. Perhaps—"

Rennert glanced at his watch.

"With your permission, Captain," he cleared his throat. "We must be starting soon. I wish to be in San Antonio by night, if possible."

"Ah, yes."

At the door Rennert met Miss Fahn.

Her face was pallid beneath a rosetted black hat, dusty from disuse. She smoothed black gloves between nervous fingers.

"Your grip is packed?"

"Yes, it is in front of my door. If you will be so kind. But be sure to handle it very carefully. I have some valuable things in it. Not breakable exactly but—well, valuable."

"Your albums?"

"Yes."

"I have been intending to tell you, Miss Fahn, about those dried flowers that you have pasted behind the postcards. What made you think they couldn't be taken into the United States?"

"Why, I always understood it was against the law to take plants into the country. They always ask you at the border if you have any plants or fruits, don't they?"

"Unless entry is prohibited by quarantine or restrictive order the importation as passenger luggage of dried herbarium specimens may be made without permit or other restriction." Rennert smiled. "I was quoting from the regulations. Just show the inspectors that you have no live plants and there will be no difficulty. They aren't by any means the ogres most people think they are."

Color came into her face.

"Oh, thank you, Mr. Rennert, for telling me. I was so afraid to risk trying to smuggle them across but I did want to take them back for our museum. They will make a collection equaled by no other in our part of the United States. And, too," her voice faltered and drifted away, "they are all that are left to me of the days I've spent here. I had such a happy time here at first. It was the first time, Mr. Rennert, that I had ever owned a place. You don't know what it means—to live all your life on the earth and never own a bit of it. Do you understand, Mr. Rennert?"

"I think I do, Miss Fahn."

Rennert's eyes went past her to the ravaged patio strewn with the mangled fragments of yesterday's flowers. He said: "Pardon me, Miss Fahn. I'll get your luggage."

"Ready to go?" Stephen Tolman called across to him. He was tall and straight, in a blue serge suit, and was swinging two bags lightly back and forth.

"Almost," Rennert told him.

He picked up Miss Fahn's heavy bulging grip and started back.

Ann Tolman came out of her room and their paths converged at the door. She fell into step beside him. Her voice was resonant with happiness: "Steve finally agreed to take that money from you, Mr. Rennert. We are considering it merely as a loan, remember. Steve insists on that. I do too, although I can appreciate your feeling with regard to it. When we get up to Santa Fe I feel sure that we shall be able to repay you in a short time."

Rennert glanced once more at the ridges of rock somewhere in whose fastnesses lay the broken remnants of a plane and the broken body of a man.

What he started to say was interrupted by a low uncertain voice from behind them. They turned.

Mark Arnhardt stood awkwardly, fumbling with unnecessary concentration at the bandage on his shoulder.

"I've told Stephen good-by, Ann—and apologized. Now I want to tell you how sorry—"

She extended a hand.

"Forget about it, Mark. Let's wish each other luck."

Their hands touched only for an instant then Arnhardt turned to Rennert.

"Good-by, Mr. Rennert." His laugh was determined. "Sorry your stay here wasn't more pleasant."

Something about his reluctance to release his pressure on Rennert's hand made the latter say: "I suppose you'll be thinking about the bright lights of Monterrey now?" It was the best he could do in the way of advice.

Arnhardt's voice was far away: "No, I think I'll stay here a while longer. I've gotten used to it, you see."

It wasn't until they had almost reached the car that Ann Tolman spoke again. She said: "Poor Mark! I wonder what he'll do? He looks so lonesome standing there in the door."

Rennert stowed away the luggage, got into the front seat beside Stephen Tolman and started the car. When they had passed under the gateway he glanced back.

Arnhardt was standing with legs apart and his thumb crooked about his belt. He wasn't looking at them any longer but straight ahead of him. Rennert recognized the rapt indrawn expression on his face and, recognizing it, speculated as to whether the hacienda Flores would change hands again.

It was an expression that he had seen so often on the faces of men as they stared day after day, with increasing self-sufficiency, into the mountains of Mexico.

The Cat Screams
ISBN 1-61646-148-9

Vultures in the Sky
ISBN 1-61646-149-7

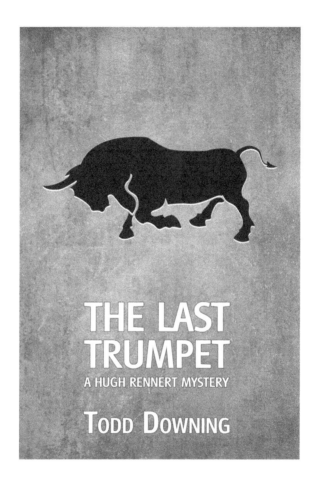

The Last Trumpet
ISBN 1-61646-152-7

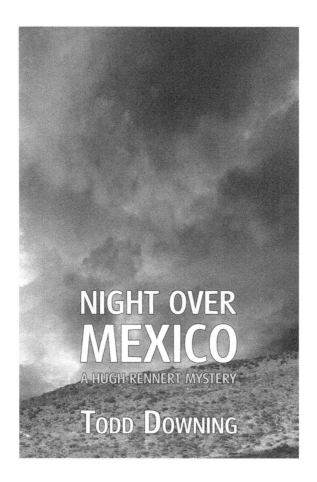

Night Over Mexico
ISBN 1-61646-153-5

Clues and Corpses: The Detective Fiction and
Mystery Criticism of Todd Downing
Curtis Evans
ISBN 1-61646-145-4